Dirt Under My Nails

Dirt Under My Nails

AN AMERICAN FARMER
AND HER CHANGING LAND

Marilee Foster

BRIDGE WORKS PUBLISHING COMPANY

Bridgehampton, New York

Published by Bridge Works Publishing Company, Bridgehampton, New York, a member of the Rowman & Littlefield Publishing Group.

Distributed in the United States by National Book Network, Lanham, Maryland. For descriptions of this and other Bridge Works books, visit the National Book Network website at www.nbnbooks.com.

FIRST PAPERBACK EDITION 2003

Line drawings by the author.

Library of Congress Cataloging-in-Publication Data

Foster, Marilee, 1970–
    Dirt under my nails : an American farmer and her changing land / Marilee Foster.—1st ed.
        p. cm.
    ISBN 1-882593-54-5 (cloth : alk. paper)
    ISBN 1-882593-77-4 (pbk. : alk. paper)
    1. Foster, Marilee, 1970–   2. Farm life—New York—Sagaponack.   3. Family farms—New York—Sagaponack.   4. Farmers—New York—Sagaponack—Biography.   5. Women farmers—New York—Sagaponack—Biography.   I. Title.

S417 .F713 A3   2002
630'.9747'25—dc21
                                                                                    2001052885

10   9   8   7   6   5   4   3   2   1

∞™ The paper used in this publication meets the minimum requirements of American National Standard for Information Sciences—Permanence of Paper for Printed Library Materials, ANSI/NISO Z39.48–1992.
Manufactured in the United States of America.

Acknowledgments

I WOULD LIKE TO THANK the *Southampton Press* for allowing me to write a weekly column that eventually became the basis for this book. I would also like to thank my mother, my frankest critic.

Prologue

I SAY I AM A FARMER BY DEFAULT.

I had finished college and on a whim thought I'd go to Maine with a friend. But 1994 was a dry, hot summer. So while my roommate went to Portland and got a job, I stayed in Sagaponack, New York, where my family has farmed for over a century. My older brother Dean and I spent the summer moving irrigation equipment from field to field. Our task, which was always pressing and at times desperate, was to "keep it raining" on what would have otherwise been three hundred acres of parched potatoes. It wasn't the first time I had worked on the farm, but it was the first time I sensed the real possibility of a place for me there.

Originally, I had gone to college with hopes of becoming a history teacher. But the professor put me to sleep so often that I decided to look into other disciplines. I am forever thankful that the woman who taught my freshman English class was both a feminist and a medievalist. She was so excited about language that her whole body got caught up in her lectures. As she slid across tables reciting Chaucer, I began to understand that a vibrant world was a connected one, one that suggested that I chase down more questions, more interesting and still obscure to me. My focus shifted and I went on to study art, creative writing, and women's studies—all three, like farming, falling far short of plotting a course to economic grandeur. I graduated from Beloit College believing I had experienced the quintessential liberal arts education and that I could now teach myself.

When a boy follows in the footsteps of a parent and takes over the family business, he is rarely asked why. Yet people who know my family still ask how and why I became a farmer. The confusion could be because I am not a man in coveralls. I wear dresses as often as I can. I say it's staying in touch with my feminine side, but the truth is I've found that no garment is better for picking tomatoes—a dress is the ideal basket.

My brother, by comparison, has always known he would farm. While I was spending summers working in ice cream parlors and horse farms, Dean was learning how to rebuild engines and drive tractors. That summer after I finished college, the two of us moved irrigation at 2 A.M., at sunrise, in pitch dark with flashlights and walkie-talkies. We joked about starting a farm-child Olympics, where best technique and time, best loading, unloading and hitching pipe were combined events. I think twenty-three minutes was our time to beat. Often I found myself in jealous awe of Dean's proficiency. Dean, like our father, chose not to go to college. Farming is a profession learned best by doing and Dean has thus learned to do almost anything. There were times, however, that I thought I could lighten his load. I thought his work would be easier if he wasn't the only "son".

Sagaponack is a beautiful place but, for farmers like us, a territory under siege. It has become part of something called the "Hamptons". And we, way out on the end of Long Island, have watched, a little dumbfounded, as our open spaces have given way to the infrastructure of an international resort. My father remembers when land went begging for eight hundred dollars an acre. Today no one blinks when house lots in Sagg sell for a million dollars or more. He is forever annoyed that he didn't buy the Rogers farm, the Cook lot or "Sczep's" piece twenty-five years ago. I know Sagg is not as beautiful as it used to be. The land my father inherited was not bounded by architectural experiments, tennis courts, or specimen trees; instead, there were hedgerows, fields, and just a few summer visitors. Today, when I ask my brother how we will cope with the ever-escalating influx of newcomers who don't know or care about our work or this area's heritage, he says, "I will tell them that summer is my season." We still talk, and always will, about packing up and leaving. But even as this place grows more expensive and less conducive to farming, the six hundred acres my family works is some of the best soil in the nation. For decades, we have done nothing but invest our energy and resources in the land; every year the roots become deeper. We rent acreage as far away as Amagansett, ten miles from home, while owning what is right out our back door. Leaving would be like cutting off limbs.

My inclination to remain in Sagg as a farmer and not a real estate agent, despite the fragility of agriculture here, is because I've found farming to be the profession with the most potential for me. Since that first summer of hauling pipe, when I thought maybe the work would keep me physically strong, the solitude keep me independent, and the variability keep me inspired, time has strengthened those sentiments. The rewards of this work are not easily explained; they come when I straighten up from hoeing or look back into the truck as it fills with potatoes and know that I have played some part in the abundance. When the ground dried up that first summer, I wasn't exactly on a career path. Now, several years later, when there are dogs pulling rats from under the barn's concrete floors, disc harrows falling apart, and harvesters breaking down, I realize I have one. Sunsets have context, as do the seedlings threading their way up through the heavy dirt. As much as I am troubled by the speeding Porsches, I accept those who cruise past as a part of my living. It is sometimes they who screech to a halt and, with their soft hands, select and buy tomatoes from my roadside stand.

Winter

A DUSTING OF SNOW that takes all day to settle makes me feel at home in December. With snow there is no reason to resent the cold. With snow the ground is luminous and night is held off. There are no shadows.

The next morning, snow gives away secrets. No one sees the cat that slips under a broken board and into the cluttered shed. It is the little footprints she leaves behind that betray her.

The guinea hens are nowhere in sight, but they too have left paths. They have scattered randomly from their coop and across the lawn. But they tend to gather about the doorways. By the side porch, the back porch, the front porch and even the glass slider, their congregation has turned the snow to slush. They shove their breasts at one another, they jockey and slip to get a better view of something inside. Perhaps themselves reflected in the glass? The polka-dotted birds will spend the day like mercury—rolling, scattering and rejoining. The seeds of frozen bittersweet and plumes of unexpected purple, the droppings of other creatures, bleed into the surface of the guinea hens' tramping.

Sagg Pond went out again last week, leaving it so low and the mud so saturated that it reflects the sky. From where I sit, I can watch twenty blue herons as they make minor flights, really suspended leaps, from one side of their statuesque neighbor to the other. They too are mirrored by the mud; every move has a mime beneath it. Herons do an inevitable lanky dance.

Really, we went almost all year without the ripe smell of mud. I, having just returned from the confines of a convention center, take deep breaths of this odor, tamping it into the bottom of my lungs. I do not consider that from where I stand at White Walls, the place where the road crosses the estuary, this effort might gag me. It does not. The cold air diminishes the stench. The waft of the drained flats provides a kind of fingerprint, a unique muck, all our own.

Though the emptiness of what was the pond has its benefits, seeing it so frequently makes me unhappy. There has been at least one public meeting on the topic of ousting the phragmites, the invasive, perennial wetland grass that surrounds the pond. It is generally agreed that the horrid reed has usurped valuable and attractive vistas. But before we go ripping them out by the roots, we should look for reasons why the non-native has successfully homogenized the pond shore. You could say that the phragmites are like corporate franchises. With diversity and energy, they have trounced indigenous competition. But we must acknowledge our part in the aggressor's success. We have unwittingly contributed to the propagation of phragmites by making the environment less and less comfortable for the native species, specifically cattails and mallows, because we dig, dig, dig our pond. Every time Sagg Pond is emptied into the Atlantic, thereby permit-

ting the incoming tides to enter, salty effusions over-
whelm the brackish marsh. Thus, the equilibrium is tilted
in favor of the phragmite, which is eager to settle in and
spread out.

Elsewhere, however, reclamation is possible. On Saturday a crew of gloved hands descended on Poxabogue
Cemetery. They tore back the overgrown edges, uncov-
ered lost stones, and the place is suddenly large and waiting. I suspect that those who have regularly passed this
burying ground have never known it was there until now.
I go there today to find the grave that has been described
to me by tombstone aficionados. Two daughters are
buried there and while they share the stone, individual
inscriptions are kept to either side, like pages of a book.
The prayer for them is shared, etched across the entire
bottom and does not heed the invisible spine. "Lie sleep
sweet babes, until we meet again . . ." The rest of the passage has sunk into the ground and I feel improper even
pressing the grass to try to read on.

TODAY, EVIDENCE OF A FAILED BLIZZARD is in the farm fields. What was forecast to be snow but turned to rain couldn't sink into the icy ground. It puddled up and froze over. With the sun shining on them, the temporary lakes are metallic, as if steel sheets were set down in the ryegrass.

One of the largest of these temporary lakes is in the field adjacent to my parents' house. When circumstances bore its creation, we kids were all happy because it gave us an alternative to our more permanent ice rink, the goose pond. The goose pond was a little depression in the backyard that my mother kept flooded for the comfort of her partially domesticated flock. Our goose pond, not unlike other small, murky bodies of water, seemed to have a gravitational pull on all us children. The surface was riddled with things you'd generally find in farmyards—cinder blocks, 2x4s, plow parts, and other miscellaneous scrap iron—all of it half submerged. It was, however, the frozen goose droppings, the seemingly most benign protrusions, that proved most hazardous. To lodge the toe of your skate in one was to come to an abrupt and complete stop, ready or not.

While this rink taught us exceptionally defensive skating techniques, we naturally longed for a wide-open space

where we might take our skating to the next level and execute more graceful transitions. When the fields froze, we
were presented with the necessary solitude and a pristine
location that, if only imagined, turned our clumsy routines
into acts of Olympic stature. The thing about these rinks
was that they were only really good for a day, two days at
most. As the water underneath inevitably receded, the ice
became thin, first at the edges and then throughout, at
places unannounced. What happened was that when you
hit these spots with narrow blades, the ice, now a membrane, let go. Your steel runners were transferred immediately to the lower level, a quasi-frozen mat of muddy
ryegrass. In better-known terminology, it is like hitting a
gravel patch on roller blades.

Initially my ankles would twist and surrender to the
sudden change. But once I realized that by maintaining momentum—if I transitioned into a run, rather than
a glide—I could stay upright. A few hasty steps as I
paddled the air for balance usually got me beyond the
weak spot, where the skates retook their intended
charge. My action was not pretty. It interrupted both
serenity and fantasy, but it introduced the reality of uncertainty, to which I first responded with adrenaline and
eventually coordination.

Recently, Southampton Town's elected officials implemented new guidelines for its comprehensive agricultural
plan, detailing how the municipality hopes to survive and
prosper, even in the face of what looks and feels like an
onslaught of people, pollution, sprawl and traffic. With
this new legislation, the officials showed how vital it is to

maintain the rural character of this place. The year, which had begun with local farmers feeling they were skating on thin ice, progressed from uncertainty to cooperation. After many months of negotiations, contentious meetings and often-emotional public hearings, the agricultural package voted on and approved on October 22, 2001, was both feasible and acceptable to the farmers. It seemed as if it would preserve the farmland on the east end of Long Island as well as the farming community itself.

The simple and wrenching irony has always been that the very thing that has made this area successful as a high-end vacation spot is called "open space". It is land abutting the Atlantic Ocean, woodland abutting farms, unobstructed vistas, peace, quiet and the occasional tractor. Open space here is largely still open space because it supports an economy—agriculture.

For as long as I can remember, I have listened and watched as my parents, along with many other farmers, have waged a constant battle for the preservation and protection of our most vital resource—unencumbered farmland. Such efforts have produced beneficial legislation. For example, there is currently an agricultural district law by which farmland is not taxed in the category of residential but rather as agricultural, at a lower rate. Until this law was implemented, local taxation was based on highest and best use evaluation, not the production of potatoes but the hypothetical production of subdivisions and cul-de-sacs. And because property is simply worth so much more if houses can be built on it, without this law, farmland owners would have been literally taxed off the land.

When the dialogue began between local government and agricultural interests, it was not nearly as constructive and flexible as it should have been. In order that Southampton Town adhere to the goal of maintaining the area's so-called rural character, it intended to adopt a new set of zoning rules. The prevailing desire is that fewer new houses will dot our landscape. The simplest and quickest way to do so is to require that all acreage of ten or more acres, when subdivided, leave 80 percent as open space.

But the plan was insufficient because it was rigid. It failed to foresee that a larger set-aside of open space, in a mansion-minded society, would not save farmland but rather establish a precedent for even larger house lots. There was no guarantee or incentive that the land reserved for crops would actually be used for crops. In the past, my brother was hired to "plant" one such agricultural set-aside. He used perennial ryegrass seed; the result was an expansive thirty-acre front lawn.

For farmers, the land is an asset, in some cases the only one they have. When the owner of farmland dies, the heirs are likely to pay huge estate taxes. A little comfort is taken in knowing that there is at least one way to pay the government and to keep the farm intact. Mostly. Though it isn't a blissful option, it is possible to subdivide the property and sell one or two parcels for development, thus raising the needed revenue or borrowing it against that liquid asset. But if the old regulations had been approved, the farm heirs would end up parting with more than they'd want. In this scenario the original acreage could very plausibly be diminished to the extent it would not be profitable or feasible to farm it. The legislation approved last October permitted farmers and farm advocates to transform what initially was seen as a "taking" from the farmers into a code that encourages both land preservation and the industry that sustains it.

Perhaps more abstract for nonfarming minds to grasp is that the original up-zoning was offensive to the very people it avowed to "save". The only property that would have been affected by this proposal was that of ten or more acres. Overwhelmingly, the only people who own ten or more acres are farmers (or retired farmers or widows of farmers who rent it to farmers) or developers. The town was asking, essentially, that farmers pay for everyone else's view while risking their own financial vitality.

The few farmers who remain here have prevailed despite the most appetizing monetary offers. They have done so because when cows weren't profitable, apples were; when potatoes waned, horses replaced them. We are landowners who, rather than fold, chose to evolve; we have improvised and continued. We have not done so because we are merely waiting for offers to get better. We do so because the success of our parents or grandparents has taught and instilled in us a desire for this kind of lifestyle. What the Southampton Town government was threatening to do would have alienated rather than included the people who uphold and maintain the bucolic backdrop by which so many other residents—builders, real estate agents, landscapers, boutique owners, pool companies and the list goes on—do very well.

Last October, the likelihood of a pitchfork rebellion was quelled by innovative and responsive governing. Rather than passing the draconian measures originally proposed, the town board listened to the farming community. Without the assistance of the Peconic Land Trust, Long Island Farm Bureau, the Group for the South Fork, and the passions of those most affected, these groundbreaking, incentive-based laws would not have been achieved.

By the nature of our profession, we farmers are able to readjust and respond to changes on many fronts, be it the weather, the market, a broken piece of machinery, or infestation of pests. We are able to tolerate this kind of instability because we are permitted certainty about one thing, that is, if all else fails, the land, which we continually pay for with our time and labor and taxes, is ours. And when it is ours, there is not only a future for farming but options.

ALTHOUGH THE RAIN IS CONFINING, I don't want it to stop. I move from window to window and see how a January thaw reveals the weakness of its season—like anything thin, undressed it cannot conceal its bones. The sparrows are tucked deep under the cedar trees. The only color I see is the putrid orange of unweathered wood, the exposed cross members of half-built houses. I don't want a purpose to drag me outside. Today, if we were young, we would play hide-and-seek. But at thirty-one, and alone in my parents' house, I ruminate about the contents of the bookshelves.

In this house the books came from my father's side of the family, the Fosters. Some were salvaged from basement floods. Many have cracked covers or pages that disintegrate when turned. There are a few in good condition—the embossed leather family Bible and practical books about things like fertilizer, boat building or caring for your firearms. A favorite is *Household Discoveries*, a book brimming with blunt advice and extreme homemade cures for all that ails, from rats to lice to colicky babies and foaling mares. Though it's not nearly as entertaining, I am also drawn to the old business ledger. In a monotonously even, flowing hand, line after line reveals who sold what, when and for how much. The information, though not particularly poetic, has historic value. The penmanship, to the extent that it looks compulsively practiced, tells me more about my grandfather than anyone living can.

All families are a combination of two—two sets of genes, two worldviews, two personalities. Cliff's family—landowners, laborers, tight-lipped. But my mother, some would say, came from an opposite world. There are piles of candid photographs—women smoking, dancing bears, babies in tin tubs, all black and white smiles against the rugged backdrop of early strip mines in South America. In the notes taken for a never completed memoir, my maternal grandmother glibly describes her husband and his family as one that was always "long on intellect and short on cash". The books that are in Dean's house are the ones that came from my mother's side. When her father died, the contents of his shelves were transferred to Dean's, not because Dean wanted them but because he had the space.

My brother has a few books of his own, but the forcibly inherited collection outnumbers and dominates. Dean's *Encyclopedia of Modern Bodybuilding* is conspicuously wedged between the chalky blue cover of *The Communist Manifesto* and the well-worn, gold and green spine of the *Scientific American's Amateur Scientist*. There are several books by Winston Churchill and the complete works of Rudyard Kipling. The biography of Genghis Khan—*The Emperor of All Men*—is right next to *The Book of Mormon*. None of this will ever interest my brother.

Throughout his life my grandfather, Jack Beattie, shifted between systems of belief. I pull a yellowed pamphlet down: "Which Church Is Right?" and tuck it back in next to Orwell's *Animal Farm*. I find a circa 1950 self-help manual, *How to Control Worry: In the Name of Common Sense*. It cost just thirty-five cents and claims, in just a few short weeks, to be able to cure that which "causes so much fear, anxiety, wakefulness, illness and marital unhappiness". There is a thin novel; the author begins with this self-deprecating dedication: "For mother, who deserved better". In the end, the book I decide to take home is *The Four Seasons, Japanese Haiku*.

I've ofteri thought I was the only person to graduate from a liberal arts college without taking a poetry class. I read, "For the haiku does not make a complete poem in our usual sense, it is a lightly sketched picture the reader is expected to fill in with his own memories." The introduction provides me with the basic rules of this poetic form, the exact number of syllables and the specific brevity that therefore requires accuracy in language. "Because the poem is tiny does not mean it is simple."

So I try to write a haiku for the day.

Gray January
The nest in forsythia
And I wait for you.

Then during the drive home I think of a hasty homage to the potholes that define our roads.

Rain breaks a surface
cold retakes and releases
Children vanish here.

Later, I write one for the beach houses.

Unescorted views
empty boxes of windows
Watch wild dogs, the sea.

THERE IS A CURIOUS CHILD OUT WALKING. She has found a stick and with it she pries up and turns over the soggy lengths of earth that the snowplows tend to leave peeled up on the side of the road. She stands up straight and hollers out, "Oh look, I've found a bug."

She and I are strangers; I can see that her adult companions are ahead and disinterested. I want to tell the little girl about the ripe goose carcass I noticed just a little further on, but at the insistence of her mother's rolling eyes, I don't. I feel an affinity for this kid. She has discovered in the damp, seemingly inhospitable environs of partially thawed mud the tenacity and availability of life. I watch as she carefully lowers the flap. Winter, I think, is like liver, always there and rich, for those who really love it.

In January, there is a pervasive little-to-do atmosphere. The distraction of holidays and holiday lights is gone. It is possible for me to go days without seeing or talking to anyone. Some feel deprived, if not depressed, by this isolation and flee to a variety of destinations, real or imagined, books or bars, Miami or Manhattan. Those who remain like it this way. And we, in turn, doubly benefit, for the same calm that sends others packing grows deeper still in their absence. There are no leaf-blowers or lawn mowers. Gone is the steady, distant hiss of highway traffic on Route 27. There are no horns, no air raid-esque security alarms, no blaring convertibles trailing opera and the stench of cigars. This month is like being in a house after the party has wound down, when the faucet drips, the clock ticks, ice melts and clinks in the bottom of a glass. In Sagg, what you'll hear now are noises generally drowned out. At night, the ocean can wake me as can the slow creak of tree limbs or the stir of a deer making her way across the lawn.

In Sagg Swamp, what's left of the snow has thawed and refrozen and, as I walk, it amplifies each step into a graceless, crashing tromp. In places where the trail crosses water, and wooden planks make bridges over the wetlands, no amount of care can stifle the groan and snap of my progress. What I know to be one, to the birds must sound like twenty clumsy nature lovers, and the sparrows needn't send out their thin whistled warning. I am heard, I am seen.

When I find a spot where I can stand, where another hiker has already collapsed the noisy snow's rafters, it doesn't take me long to discover that this morning belongs to the woodpeckers. They are everywhere, sending loud, hollow raps throughout the woods. A Downy Woodpecker works its way down and around the limb of a dying tree. It insistently raps and chisels out the life that's left—the unlucky, slow-moving bugs, a hearty meal.

I hear a gnawing noise and look up to see that a chipmunk has come out on the sunny side of his oak dwelling. It is eating a nut, turning it gently with its dexterous paws, like it's greedily contemplating a little jewel. When we make eye contact, it lowers its breakfast and freezes. We stare, I blink, and the chipmunk darts back into its hole. From somewhere out of sight I hear a chickadee's precocious scold. And the repetitious, drawn-out *tsk, tssk, tssssk,* the come-no-closer warning of the wren. The nuthatch has a slightly nasal honk. It brings levity to the fact that every creature here is telling me I don't belong.

The swamp is at the head of Sagg Pond. I can hear the muffled volley of the hunters' guns, and I know, beforehand, that a flock of ducks will be heading in soon. Sagg Swamp is a protected nature preserve. It is one of the tenuously connected little ponds and bogs that dot a path for wildlife from here to Sag Harbor, the northern side of the Island's south fork. At the center of the swamp is an inaccessible (to most) pond, called Jeremy's Hole—the name supposedly taken from the tenant farmer's boy who ran away, and because they only found his buttons in the mud, was thought only to have gotten that far. I imagine Jeremy's Hole is like a safe house, popular with mallards and geese. A flock of mallards circles above, they slow and set their wings, then the entire flock drops at the same time, but in certain separate airspaces. One who has fallen behind—could have been shot at, nearly killed—now careens into view. It's trying to catch up and losing altitude so fast that its wings rip through the air; a little span of feathers roars with the composed resistance of a jet airplane.

Crows fly past, alight in high trees and then mob back the other way. If they do not have a predator—a house cat or a fox to harass—then the crows turn the witch hunt on one another. They dive and torment. Over this cacophony comes a lone and sharp high note, so clear and sobering that while I wait for it to repeat, I lose awareness of all the other sounds. It is probably the hermit thrush. Though the bird is common to this area, it is as reclusive as its name implies. Often it is only the thrush's pretty, simple noise that tells you it's there. The swamp, as the thrush hesitates, falls silent again.

Just as my eyes will roam a room occupied by faces, pausing and assigning traits to utter strangers, so too do the ears love a promenade. The swamp is one such place, but there are others. At Sagg Main Beach between the ocean and the pond, just before the sun goes down, a short-eared owl moves through looking for his dinner. I hear a ruffle as he leaves his perch in the cedar tree, unfolds his silent wings and becomes a silhouette, swooping high, then low. The only noise I hear in all this activity is the wind pushing the phragmites. From the backside of the dune, I can look across the pond, count three herons wading near the tide-nipped peninsula of Smith Corner. Out on the mudflat a group of seagulls maul a carp that has frozen and curled up, crescent moon–shaped. Bufflehead ducks practically run across the water, necks out, wings flapping, tiny flocks quarreling over the territorial placement of invisible lines. Sparrows, always nearby, reduce themselves to blurs; they retreat to depths of the thorny beach rosebush and wait until I am past. As if a hand grabbed and stopped a metronome, an occasional smack of a wave interrupts the pond's persistent, soft lap.

IT IS THAT TIME OF YEAR. Winter has lost its earlier invigorating charm, and there is nothing to mask the changes—no foliage to hide behind, no colors to distract my eyes. I notice the silence because the frozen grass is loud as it snaps underneath my feet.

Most of us who spend our winters here also spend our summers here. The same cannot be said for those who spend their summers here. Yet. I have friends who came to terms with the fact that if they had to share this place in the summer, at least they'd get the balance of the year, October to April, to enjoy in empty, languid bliss. But each year it seems that there are more and more part-timers who linger. Labor Day is no longer a vacuum. What began as *doing Thanksgiving in the country* or *popping out for a few weekends around Christmas* led naturally to a slow and steady buildup of unfamiliar faces on a regular basis. I know there are fewer and fewer physical differences between those who have always and those who haven't always lived in Sagaponack. Some year-rounders say that New Yorkers are pushier, but this is hard to gauge; people are pushy, period. The symptoms just get worse when you crowd them in cities or in general stores that are small, like ours, just down the street.

In Sagg, as in any place on earth, the longer you live here, the more convincingly you believe you know the place. After years of being here I believe I could recognize anywhere that Sagaponack smell of dying potato vines, empty pond basins and seaweed drying slowly in the sun. I know quiet features like runaway ponies and low-lying fog. There are things I know about Sagg that I like to keep all to myself, but there are also those that should be shared. Everyone who comes to Sagg and decides to stay needs to be told the premise of the name. "Saga-what?" says the mail-order taker. I am happy when people can pronounce or spell Sagaponack because the next thing they generally say is, "What does that mean?" The fact that Sagg has an oddball name translates into the more important point. In Sagaponack, there is something you can't find everywhere.

Last summer we hauled three moldy books from my brother's basement. Dean lives in the house we all grew up in. And before us, my grandparents Charles and Ann Foster raised their family there. Ever since Dean moved in, we have from time to time orchestrated an effort to rid the house and my brother from the yoke of familial packrats. The books, volumes one, two and three, *A History of Long Island*, by William S. Pelletreau, published 1903. I opened one and scanned the index for Sagaponack. I opened another to read this familiar entry, only the spelling is slightly different:

Saggaponack is the general name for all the land east of Sagg pond. It is of Indian origin and signifies, "the place where the biggest ground nuts grow" and has always been accounted the most fertile land in [Southampton] town.

While Sagg's vegetable economy has averaged out to become more diverse, it used to be a lot heavier with potatoes. The assumption was that since the potatoes did so well in Sagg, "ground nut" could only mean the abundant spud. However, historical research proves this hypothesis wrong. While the potato did originally come from the New World, it was only the Inca who cultivated and ate the vegetable. When that empire was turned under, the Spanish took the potato back to Europe—but it was not considered a treasure. Europeans were suspicious of something that grew out of sight and they kept the tuberous vegetable at a safe distance. It is believed that the potato made it back across the Atlantic, this time landing on the East Coast, where it was cultivated as fodder for livestock and food for slaves. Potatoes are not native to Long Island, much less Sagaponack, and it is therefore unlikely that the ground nut mentioned in the old volume has anything to do with a vegetable that wouldn't thrive here for another couple of hundred years.

It is more likely that the ground nut was one of our indigenous weeds. Nut sedge, or as it is more commonly known, nut grass, thrives here. If you don't keep after it, it will spread, its tentacle-like roots weaving a white carpet under the peas. Above ground, a sharp reedlike grass closes in and chokes out rows of carrots, beans and cucumbers. Even tall crops, like corn, have succumbed to a nut grass infestation. The nut of the nut grass is its seed; it resembles a hazel nut, only elongated, and shriveled with a brown papery wrapper. I know people who have eaten these seeds—or at least tried to. The noxious nut, though excessively plentiful in our soil, is bitter and mildly poisonous.

We cannot discount the possibility that the nut the Native Americans so approvingly named Sagaponack for could have been harvested into extinction. We may never know the exact truth, and yet this should not rob us of a historical identity. I have come to believe in my relatively few years of farming that it is not so much the type of nut as it is the attribute of legendary size. One year I grew a watermelon that weighed eighty-one pounds. I nearly put my back out picking it; it was the size of a full-grown hog. The most prominent issue here is that we, as Long Island's earliest inhabitants, were and are continually awed by this soil's fertility and its ability to grow things noticeably bigger.

My worry, of course, is that Sagg's future inhabitants will look around as I once looked around and, based on what they see, reinterpret "land of the large ground nuts" to mean something altogether different. I fear and do not doubt a coming day by which we aren't known for our potato yields or weed patches, but for other grandiose nuts, the cedar-shingled kinds, clustered as subdivisions or sprawling behind the hedges like isolated little kingdoms.

ON A RAINY SUNDAY, Sagaponack and all her guinea hens are wet. Their charcoal feathers hang askew around their bony ankles like soggy, polka-dotted dancing gowns. Rather than seek shelter, as other birds have, they haunt our lawn, the roadside and Bob Dash's dormant gardens. While rain takes a heavy toll on the hens' exotic good looks, the weather hardly alters their consistently strange behavior. After years of keeping these birds as "pets" we have decided that eye-catching as they may be, they have no cerebral capacity for memory. Every task—flying over the fence or descending from their treetop roosts (they come blazing through the branches like they've never flown), or warding off dogs or navigating the sometimes lethal traffic on Main Street—must be done each day with new ambition. The guinea hens are curious, loud and easily alarmed.

We also have a hen turkey. Earlier this year she defected from her flock and her heritage to join the guinea hens on their daily exploits. Since the turkey is often regarded as one of the most intelligent birds, we cannot understand why she'd want to hang out with a flock of intellectually inferior fowl, assimilating their behavior for her own. But she is, of course, still a turkey and this is more evident during these cold downpours; the native

North American bird doesn't look so miserably frumpy as her sub-Saharan companions. From where I sit at the kitchen table, I can see the group come out of the asparagus patch. The guineas flit about like a bunch of ill-equipped debutantes; the turkey, in her simple, sturdy plumage, struts.

There are very few things, like our mismatched flocks, that come out and stay out in weather like this. Days like this are why we have bowling, matinees and, more recently, sport utility vehicles. These sensational additions to our roadways conquer with size and impact all that threatens to restrain them—including common sense. I watch as one careens past—a dark blue Range Rover. I've driven in enough "lottie cars" to know exactly what's going on in the Range Rover. The passengers are squealing with delight and goading the driver on. With a quick, if not suave, jerk of the driver's wrist, the car sweeps from the center of the road to the edge, where puddles have taken shape. The vehicle disappears into a spray of four muddy rooster tails. It reappears on the yellow line, just in time to dive right. But this won't be a simple parting of the Red Sea; this is a puddle that aims to keep. The vehicle begins to hydroplane. I know the squeals have gone plaintive. Life itself flashes before the passengers' eyes as the rear and front end of that boxlike compartment wrench in opposite directions. But like a gunshot, as suddenly as the skid begins, it stops. The car, modeled after the ideal gentleman, knows just how to terrify before stepping in and retaking the helm in a more sober fashion. The SUV rights itself, regains composure, slows, puts on its blinker and takes the left fork toward

Gibson Beach. The driver tries to muster a convincing "scared ya, didn't I" grin and two of the three passengers giggle, embarrassed they'd ever doubted.

I know why the car almost capsized. By the side of the road there is a drainage ditch, perhaps the lowest point on Sagg Main. When the puddles are one inch deep, the ditch is already full and flowing back into the road. If it were spring, and I were twenty years younger, that drainage ditch would look inviting. We used to swim in it as early as April. The ditch was different then, more like a ramp, and so when it was full of water it had a deep and shallow end. It wasn't as frequently used as a landfill, nor did it have a sign in the middle, UNLAWFUL TO DUMP. When I remember swimming there I remember two things: the quality of the water and being cold. Water that washed a quarter mile down Main Street was colored by the purple and green swirl of petroleum products. The pool wasn't filled by road runoff only but with what ran off horse pastures and farm fields. The water was thick with topsoil. When we got home from the swimming ditch, we could wring silt out of our drenched clothing. Cars waved when they went by; sitting where I sit now, my mother would gaze at us in amused·disbelief with her hand under her chin. We came home when our lips turned blue and stood outside the back door as she guarded the entrance, gave us towels, and ordered, "Clothes off! Clothes off!"

FOR MUCH OF THE WEEK the ocean has been raging. It took away the coffer-dam that someone built in front of a house on Scott Cameron Beach. Of all the things people do to save their oceanfront homes, this one had been the most sensational we'd seen in years. It was an attraction, it was almost art, the kind of sculpture you can touch, a monument. It rose out of the low tide mark in successive tiers of nylon mesh packed tight with trucked-in sand. We could walk out on the dam or run up and down on it as if it were giant steps from the sea. It was made to emulate the dune that had originally buffered the property from the ocean, and for a while, the artificial one did its job. But the very high tide finally succeeded in working the edges loose (though some claim it was sabotage). Once this happened, sand began to drain from the mesh and more and more water got in, until it yanked the seawall out of position. A color aerial photo in the local paper shows the costly barricade slumped at the foot of the house, and a sandbar made of its innards streams west toward the inlet of Mecox Bay.

I can hear the ocean from the farm; my father can gauge storms by its roar. Houses aren't the only things that suffer in bad weather around here. Lately the ocean has been taking what's left of Gibson Beach's dune banks. Before houses were built behind them and they became private property, the dunes were all I knew of mountain ranges. My sister could vanish in them. To make the summit was an exhilarating trek up a steep, sandy grade. Once at the top, we turned to run back down. By halfway, the momentum would overtake the body's coordination. If you were lucky, you could turn this potential disaster of leg and limb into a series of death-defying somersaults. It was only whiplash you had to look out for.

I probably understood the word "erode" before I could spell "erase" and it wasn't just that as I got bigger, the dunes got smaller. Snow fences went up to keep us out. Little signs, "Help control erosion, do not walk on the dunes," were everywhere, until staying off was protocol. While I wouldn't know how to prove it, it does seem that when homes go up behind the dunes, the dunes tend to drift away more quickly. At a cocktail party last summer a drunken man, using his hands, explained how the dunes are built from the back. One hand is the wind as it sweeps up the back of the dune, one hand is the ocean pushing the other way. One hand is the house that changes the air flow, the sand flow. "Traps the flow," he says and then gestures downward, his hands—the house and the dunes spiraling out of sight—like he's completed some magic trick.

Memories visit like the friends you didn't invite, but who drop by anyway. To your delight or dismay, they'll sit there corrupting solitude. I stay inside, no television, no book or radio, listening to the rain beating on the skylight like the soundtrack for a biblical flood. Every subject turns into reverie. And since the past, set in time and place, doesn't have any more permanence than the present, I cannot arrive at a place and stop. My recollection of the dunes—bigger and better than they now are—has been replaced. Today, without seeing, I know the tide frolics, sticks out its tongue, tasting the foolishly built chateau's front porch. Impediments be damned.

IT MAY INTEND TO PROMOTE LOVE, but Valentine's Day often stirs less benevolent emotions. There is wrath to contend with, scorn to express, sorrow to swell and break the meniscus of decency. Nasty breakups are seldom walked away from with ease. This counterproductive conduct doesn't only apply to the regular intimacies between two people, but locally when a resident professes to love the ocean so dearly, to need her so much, that he must build a house as an homage on the weave of her shifty hemline.

Last week as many were preoccupied with amorous thoughts, the ocean was brooding, slowly climbing steadily from small into bigger fits until, just west of Peter's Pond, she took an entire house into the raging tide. When the ocean wants to break up with one of her lovers, we all hear about it. Workmen come to cut off the gas and electric, moving vans fill with salvaged furniture and appliances. For some the situation is a convenient blend of education and entertainment. We clamber to the beachfront by the hour to assess the progress and debate the impact of the next high tide, which will be higher than the previous one. Bets are taken—when the stairs will go, when the pool will go, when the foundation will crumble and the waves will finally crest over a sinking, shingled roofline. People flock from the surrounding towns; old men who haven't been to the beach, much less Sagaponack, in years drive the six miles from Sag Harbor to offer their opinions.

When contemporary beach houses fall into the sea, I compare it to the bitter divorce that often comes at the end of an exaggerated romance, one that friends and neighbors and even strangers in restaurants saw coming. The house is so steeped in promises and lavish embellishments that when it crumbles, an equally intense afterlife of literally washed-up dreams and litigation begins. When one pays many millions for such a rare perch, the buyer cannot help but consider the property his own, with no premonition that it might be temporary. The local government does little to dissuade the delusion. There may be a few environmental restrictions, but the owner is largely permitted to build whatever he likes. Houses reminiscent of gothic castles, Tuscan villas and erector set experiments flourish. Beachfront property, though it continues to be the most unstable, has become the most expensive investment. Property taxes are levied not on the geological fallibility of the property but on the real estate market's assessment. Thus the owner is led to believe that his valuable plot of land is of concern to, and under the care and protection of, the government. If, by acts of time and nature that property is diminished, the owner expects action, compensation and compassion. He doesn't anticipate that when he wants to dump an abutment of boulders where his deck once was, he'll be met with small-town, bureaucratic impediments—a public hearing, an environmental impact statement. Because it is not possible to sue Mother Nature, the town board is charged instead with negligence, indecision and poor planning.

As the popularity of this place has boomed, people with no historic ties have moved here. Since they did not grow up with photo albums and stories recounting what a "real" storm can do, these newcomers are sometimes lacking a healthy fear of the Atlantic. Instead, they are infatuated with the sea, thus mistaking the placid days as always attainable beauty and reciprocal affection. But the seasons treat the beach differently. In winter, when our weather is out of the north, the ocean always takes bites out of the beach. The following spring, she'll redeposit it, though maybe not in its entirety and not generally in the same place. Erosion is a drawn-out game of musical chairs, an axiom of coastal communities. Losing your spot is as obvious as it is unchangeable.

Before my mother married a "local", she was a girl from New Jersey whose family spent their summers in Sagg, sleeping two to a cot in a beach house or, as it came to be called, "the shack". It was the legacy of a distant relative, Uncle Matt, who in 1910 rented a dune, with permission to "erect a camp" on the south end of Fairfield Pond, overlooking the ocean. The agreement cost him five dollars.

From the pictures I have seen, it *was* a shack. The beach house, like all the others of that era, was made of crude but sturdy design, out of found and recycled building materials (often the debris of shipwrecks). Fifteen by twenty feet, the shack had one door and three windows.

The roof leaked. Sparrows made their nests on the inside. It was just one room, tucked behind the dune bank, divided at the children's bedtime by blankets draped over one of the three rafters. It was little more than a fortified tent: nothing to walk your friend through or hire landscapers to tend.

Until fairly recently, it was common knowledge that anything built close to the ocean was not an item of permanence. To compare the house my mother knew with those built today is to consider the difference between a duck blind and the Sydney Opera House; one is practical, taking its environment into serious consideration, the other, forged of rock, iron, glass and wood, espouses and houses extravagance and high art. The shack gave access to summer fun and refuge from thunderstorms; it was never thought of as anything more splendid.

Those bygone shanties were always a work in progress, their incarnations and alterations based largely on the weather. Just as a storm might take away the platform that had served as a front porch, so might a second storm provide a much needed door. Thus, scavenging the beach before, during and after the onset of foul weather was a resourceful challenge—an obligatory but creative part of summer. Storms could also be credited with the slow migration of the houses themselves. My mother's started at Fairfield Pond but successive hurricanes swept and lodged the house steadily westward. The shack was behind the dunes at Sagg Main Beach in the spring of 1961, when an equinoctial gale finally finished it off.

I do not doubt the extent of my mother's and her family's attachment to the shack. My grandmother painted it numerous times, and the impression her watercolors give me is of both whimsy and reverence for a tiny and flimsy stronghold. It was their small bit of paradise, and yet when the ocean washed it apart for the final time there was nothing to salvage and rebuild on. Theirs was a quiet and resolute separation with memories intact. For sure there was a sense of loss—my mother has a certain piece of driftwood framed—but there were no regrets.

STORMS OF LENGTH AND INTENSITY scour the atmosphere. They blow and pummel the impurities out of the sky and today, the day after such a storm, is perfect, despite the cold, for a long and investigative beach walk. With the tide receded, the ocean is flattened out, barely able to consume its own undertow, seeming both demure and blameless. From the fated mansion, we find lightbulbs and parts of a living room chair. There is a sofa, half buried but still good for sitting on, at Gibson Beach. A woman opens her hands, bright pink from the cold, and shows me the remnants of an oceanfront garden. She holds an assortment of daffodil and daylily bulbs and thinks perhaps they've survived the drowning and will do better in her safer backyard.

No matter what they say about the truncated month of February, with each day growing noticeably longer, it still has a way of being endless. Unlike later and more true spring months, February can afford to slide back on all of its advances. There are no prescribed transitions; if something doesn't get done here, it can be put off 'til March. And if March doesn't get it done, well, there is still April. February doesn't love the start of grape hyacinths, the greening catbrier, the skunk cabbage. It is a month that tolerates change but makes growth look painful, like teeth when they punch up through a glassy red gum.

A grackle landed all alone in the backyard, driving the blue jays from the feeder. It is common and cruel. It crosses the yard with the air of a dictator who fancies himself an esteemed, legitimate royal figure, wearing dark, velvety feather robes. Its beady eyes catch me behind the glass door watching, and as with all its subjects and all its invisible territory, the inspection is hasty and contemptuous. The grackle is home now and no human is to be trusted. The bare maple trees fill with black birds. The first starlings to arrive snatch up the deep and tidy nests, the ones built by flickers last year. With birds, mortgages are not responsible for migration.

Vegetable seeds arrive in boxes and I sort them, rubber-band them: beets and spinach, carrots and chard, separated by the week they are to be sown. I put them in the back porch almost out of sight and wish for just a little more winter.

LAST WEEK MY FAMILY went to Syracuse because the New York State Agricultural Society gave my father, Cliff, the Century Farm Award. The award is public and important enough to rate a bronze plaque and a proclamation signed by the governor.

Awards are like compliments or even insults: from whence they come is what makes them relevant. The Agricultural Society was established in 1832, its mission then, as it is now, to serve the individuals and families who are committed to keeping productive agriculture alive and well. This society initiates and sponsors many good works, from agricultural fairs to collegiate scholarships. The philosophy behind its Century Farm Award is to honor those people who have exhibited the resourcefulness that permits their farms to meet and exceed the demand of an ever-changing market. In addition, the award calls specific attention to a "century farm", a farm that has been in the same family, passed from one generation to the next, for at least one hundred years.

In my father's case, the farm was inherited from his father, Charles, in 1957. Charles and his brother, Everett, had inherited the farm from their father, Clifford J. Foster, who had in turn inherited it from his father, Josiah, in 1880.

Josiah's gravestone leans against our garage. It is white marble, about three feet tall, and we don't know how or why it's here and not where he is interred. We can only assume that for some reason the stone was brought back to the descendants and some thrifty person then set it, facedown, as an entryway for one of the farm's work sheds. Years later, when the shed was being renovated, the stone was rediscovered, brushed off and placed upright.

Josiah Foster was a whaling captain. A few letters written home give us what seems to be a very honest account of a man who had ridden the high and was now watching not only his great industry, but also the creatures it profited from, in rapid decline. And though these letters are not much more than personal asides, we have Josiah's reveries. Such thoughts, which even the most conscientious letter writer can avoid, are penned when the writer is horribly homesick. Whaling crews, especially as whales became more scarce, were at sea for three or more years. These voyages were extended in hopes that time and luck might eventually run together and make the endeavor profitable. While anchored off Baja California, Captain Foster wrote to his brother William,

> We come over here to get a kind of whale which heretofore has been but little taken as they are much smaller whale than Right whales and their oil is not worth quite as much. But as other whaling has failed and so poor, we poor whalemen are glad to get any kind of oil and where ever we can. The whales average about 30 barrels and are a very ugly whale to take. Many men are

killed and hurt by them. I believe there is no labor or business that is so wearing as whaling and if the good Lord spares my life to get home once more whaling will never trouble me again. Whales are so very scarce and small to what they were some six and ten years ago.

He doesn't go on at any length about his own temperament while at sea, but he does write of the sailors who abandon ship and hence we infer a little more of Josiah's disposition. While he admits conditions are bad, nothing is worse than the wretched sailors who steal boats only to die, for the Baja coast is nothing but a desert. He reasons, if the sailors are not punished by the gruesome details of their deaths, justice will come later.

If I could have caut [sic] them they would be sorry that they ever see Cap J Foster but perhaps they are now in the hands of One who will reward and punish more justly than I can. I want to get home once more and get clear of sailors.

In 1870, when he was forty-three, Josiah left whaling. And as he had most desired (in a letter to his wife, Mary), he bought a plot of land in Sagaponack and moved his family there. Josiah became a farmer, but we do not know much about his successes or failures. He died just nine years later and sometime within those nine years, the original farmhouse burned down.

What I like about the real and imagined Josiah Foster was that he, the first farmer of my heritage, was also the one who knew a contrasting occupation. As a sea captain, he bemoaned his exhaustion and a job that was thankless and dangerous and ambiguously governed as much by luck as it was by hard work. In his letters, he contends over and over again that his is an occupation that only prayer and God's mercy will see him through. And, interestingly, he envisions farming as a break from the wearisome trials of man against man, sea and beast. Two hundred years later, my family has very much the same to say of farming.

Josiah's eldest son, Clifford, my father's namesake and grandfather, inherited the farm when he was twenty-two. Josiah at age fifty-three had fallen from a haymow, and after languishing for six months, died. All I know of Clifford J. Foster is that it was he who most heavily influenced my own father. When my father speaks of his grandfather, he'll say things like, "Now he, he was a real farmer," and he'll say this with both hands raised up and spread wide, not so much in a preacher's reverent gesture but rather as if he were presenting a special box to an awestruck audience. Understand that my father is not liberal with compliments, and so such an utterance both haunts and inspires me . . . I have such relatives. When my father says "real" his gaze is not heaven-bound but leveled at me or my brother, or at some other aspiring farmer who happens to be sitting across from him. He uses the word "real" to make an important distinction, because for as long as man has sought his fortunes in professions that are divorced from the earth, so too has he longed (perhaps idealistically) to return to the earth's compliant folds. My father knows this: there are two kinds of farmers.

Word has long been out about the fertile soils of Long Island's East End. A visitor here need only peruse the farm stands that dot our back roads and highways, or gaze out his farm-view picture windows to be convinced that such an abundance is easily attained. It is not an uncommon thing to see a lawyer, doctor or financier in the "Hamptons" donning his first "Nothing runs like a Deere" cap. This area, with its unsegregated country-mouse, city-mouse communities, is a perfect breeding ground for something called a "flash in the pan" farmer. The local newspapers often write about that pioneering spirit who gave up a six-figure job and all of life's superficialities to get a little dirt under his nails and reinvigorate his soul. Sometimes both happen, which suits him just fine until he realizes he is working harder than he ever did, and with less financial return. What's more, his new occupation is eating into his retirement fund faster than he had calculated. Often the "wanna-be" sells all his equipment, converts or rents his land and goes back to not-being a farmer, with maybe a not-so-much reinvigorated soul but a wiser one.

My great-grandfather was a real farmer not because we know anything about his agricultural practices, crop yields or innovative equipment modifications but because we know he was a resource and a leader in the agricultural community. He provided seeds, fertilizers and encouragement to those who were just starting out. Many of these farmers, having emigrated from Ireland and Poland, arrived here with very little money and even less security. This sort of explains why Clifford J. ended up as the president of the

Sag Harbor Savings Bank. He knew that agriculture could thrive here and he found ways to assist and secure other farmers in their profession.

Though he may not openly admit it, my father, though not a banker in a formal sense, has emulated his grandfather in other ways. Frustrated as he may get with incompetence, he is the first to attempt to lead someone out of it. He loves to teach and invent, and he is willing to advise anyone who comes asking—not only about farming, but about the pitch of a roof, the grade of a driveway, plumbing, electrical work, hydraulics, welding and steam engines. He knows how things work and most of his understanding has been through experience.

Still he considers himself "hard luck". In trying moments and in farming there is much of that; an entire day can line up beginning to end with everything going wrong. A mistake early in the day can have exponential impact on progress. The delay of a dead battery is followed by a rush that leads to an overloaded primary chain on the digger which in turn causes the whole thing to "wrap", and we need an extra hour, the one we just lost, to fix it. My father is the first to cuss himself. He'll say he should never have gotten out of bed, then call himself a broke-down, dumb farmer. He'll wish himself dead and gone. But because, in the end, none of what he says is true, nothing charms my father more than salvaging what the untrained eye would consider a lost cause. And not only does he fix the machine, he mends the broken part so that it will never break again. When he put beams under the old farmhouse, he used I-beams that could have supported a high-rise. I have always known that my father is the last to congratulate himself. I suppose humility is an integral, if not superstitious, part of farming. If you let your guard down long enough to pat yourself on the back, you're not being responsible and you'll pay in the end.

But in Syracuse, on the occasion of the Century Farm Award, the convention center was filled with people who, like him, had figured and fussed, risked and rerigged until they had arrived at the most efficient solution. The audience and the recipient therefore had a common understanding of what it really means to keep a farm and its family running. It is a task not exclusive to the fifty or so years it is up to him to sustain; it comes with both a legacy and an expectation that the farm will not expire when he does. His audience realistically appreciated what my father can do and therefore could honestly applaud his hard work. Thus the award, which he felt "funny, almost guilty about receiving", was made meaningful to us all.

WITH FEW EXCEPTIONS, winter out here is consistent. You know who you pass. You know what cars will be parked at the post office, who's going to talk to you, who's not. So when something happens late in February—when all the corridors of information are completely empty, word travels very fast. It can seem as if you heard what happened before it even has.

Early Thursday morning in the vicinity of our farm, at least a dozen men could be seen scurrying from barn to barn, back and forth across the road. By ten, cars were slowing at the end of our driveway, and neighbors who could have come in, peered in. What might have looked like an invasion of bearded men in straw hats and wearing slightly undersized black suits was only an Amish crew hired to install six new barn doors.

It is a growing consensus among farmers that if you need something for your farm, you'd be better off driving to Pennsylvania than spending the time and extra money ordering or affording it here. Farmers from Long Island see more of each other in Lancaster County perusing the aisles of the Tractor Supply Company than we do locally at places like K-mart. Hardware stores in Pennsylvania are different; you can buy water troughs and plowshares, tractor springs, and batteries that can run an entire dairy. Every time my father and I set foot in one and emerge with our arms brimming with agricultural goodies, I hear the same lament, "It's too bad we don't have one of these back home." The simple fact is that "back home" there are no longer enough farms to warrant Ace Hardware trying to sell salt licks and cultivator shoes at competitive prices. So we buy our tractors in Pennsylvania, our extension cords, our lag bolts, water tanks, our hydraulic oil and boot socks that won't shimmy around your ankles. The overhead doors are just one more product my father found faster and cheaper just two states to the west, and the Amish installation was part of the deal.

If you think of your average automatic garage door and multiply it by eight, this is about the size of the door to our largest barn. The men worked for two days straight; they went to a local diner for supper and got sick; they brought cots and slept in the heated, but not particularly warm, barn. The contact our modern society has with the Amish is somewhat monopolized and controlled by those who have a vested interest in keeping the veil of illusion opaque. We see postcards of young girls heading into white schoolhouses. We do not see the Amish man lighting a Marlboro and leaning out of his carriage to offer one to his buddy. But it happens, just as we don't see Amish boys, allegedly chaste in the ways of time-saving power tools, handling the "Sawzall", the Makita drills, the impact wrench. They use these implements with confidence and dexterity. Over the years, as my father has made friends and become better acquainted with several Amish merchants, we have come to understand something about Pennsylvania's most industrious population. They might frown on owning such tools, but borrowing them is a permitted and blissful luxury.

I CAN'T HELP NOTING that it is almost March and my first pair of fully insulated Carhartt overalls still hang stiff and clean. Their purchase was like a rite of passage and I had so looked forward to breaking them in. It has been too warm to justify their use and now, nearly at winter's end, they have no grease stains, no corn rolled in their cuffs. Essentially they have no life story and this is depressing.

I am also depressed to see the perennials mistake the unseasonable warmth for the early spring it mimics. An additional aspect unsettles me because it's a break in tradition. For the first time in collective memory, we removed the Christmas lights, all thirty-six strands of them from the fifty-foot, and still growing, fir tree on the village green. The tree was planted in memory of Warren Topping. His sons, Alvin and Bud, planted it at the cemetery green the year after Warren died. Alvin keeps the bittersweet out, and Bud enlists the help of my father— one of his oldest friends—and Dean too, to help light it. The tree is so big Dean spends the better part of two days up in the bucket of a "cherry picker"—the kind of trucks electrical companies use. We borrow a crane for the very top. It's a feat to decorate, and much like the indoor trees, much harder to undo, but this year with no excuses like biting wind and bitter cold, Dean felt obligated. After all, the practice of leaving the lights on and hoping they'll be okay the following year has improved nothing but soldering skills.

I find myself worried when winter has no real impact. When it feels like a slow roll of uncommitted freezes and a warm spell, I am suspicious of its real intentions. Will winter resurge later, when we most expect it to end? Nice, go-and-be-outdoors weather interrupts the time I prefer to spend in hermetic productivity with temperature-induced logical lapses; I want to plant radishes. While I have a few friends who point to this balmy condition as proof of global warming, the majority I meet are more concerned with their own symptoms—stuffy nose, achy bones, incessant coughing fits.

ILLNESS GOT A HOLD ON ME last week—first came a short temper, then chills, fatigue and finally gridlocked nasal passages. During the siege I was offered many remedies. Curing colds, like digging holes or skinning cats, is a highly opinionated science. It is funny that we should continue to refer to the viral predator as "common", for our avenues of defense are anything but.

Most everyone agrees that there is no such thing as the early detection of a cold; the moment you feel a dry tickle in your throat it is too late for sleep and vitamin C. Now the only variable you have any control over is the severity of the onslaught and how long the convalescence. Any product that pledges to "suppress" a cold generally weakens it but ultimately prolongs the malady.

Alcohol is the remedy for a chest cold and a head cold, according to a southern friend—alcohol even if you're running a fever. She laces her lemon tea with a shot of bourbon. Her theory is to get the sufferer both heated up and sleepy. Once resting under an excessive pile of blankets, your body will sweat both the booze and the sickness out of its system.

Many, with involuntary wincing expressions, remembered how their mothers slathered Vicks Vapo-Rub on their necks, under their noses, across their chests, and even in their armpits. I shall never forget the burning cool that bonded me to my nightie. Yet, even with this discomfort, the eucalyptus glob did have a magical property by which the lodged was loosened. After a Vicks rub-down, I could lie on my back and take long, deep breaths. There are concoctions that, if they don't work one way, will work in another. If an onion crushed and hung in a porous bag around the neck fails to cure a cold, at least the stench will have effectively quarantined the infected. In cases of extreme sore throats, the sweetened juice of an onion is said to wash down the infection.

We shouldn't forget that the common cold is often accompanied by unattractive side effects other than sniffling. Serious, bedridden bouts inflict not just pallor but fever blisters. Colds, because they force you to breathe through your mouth, dry and chap lips. A cure for these oral discomforts is credited to the questionably enlightened, but innovative enough, doctors of the Middle Ages. They found that one's own earwax could subdue the ugly ruptures.

By far the most drastic remedy for the common cold traces its roots to South Carolina. Norman, a man who has worked for my dad since my dad started out, tells me how his mother would work down the lineup of him and his siblings with spoonfuls of sugar doused with kerosene. She muttered reassuringly as she went—wiping the spoon on her apron—from one crying mouth to the next: "If you can catch a cold, then you ought to be able to kill it."

Spring

I CAN'T RECALL if our friend the groundhog saw his shadow this year. Even if I could, I've never been able to remember the rules of the ritual. Shadow equals an early spring or shadow equals a late one? It is more important to know, in farming anyway, that one should not count on a furry, burrowing animal to predict the weather. No matter when or how spring arrives, it is a temperamental season with an undisclosed number of days into which a farmer must fit a somewhat specific schedule. So March is spent in preparation. It is conceivably the last chance a farmer will have to imagine obstacles rather than confront them.

Most other professions are not tethered to the seasons. Many would just as soon take the shifty, unreliable month right out of the calendar, erase it like the thirteenth floor. March is a month of reprieve without respite; nothing's started and nothing's doing. Just one holiday, though not the one that closes banks and post offices and not one for the kids to get excited about, just a day to get drunk and wear green—even if it doesn't match your shoes. So it is little wonder that March, with its generally disagreeable climate, its long and windy afternoons, incites anxiety and restlessness—the base catalyst for spring cleaning.

When the urge to tidy up takes hold of my friend Stephanie, she kneels on the kitchen countertops pulling stale tea and rusty cans of noodle soup from the cabinets. She uses her pink sponge like a broom, cursing, gently sweeping mouse "dirts" out of the corners. Lawrie, feeling a need for more space, gives back to the Salvation Army all the outfits she has purchased there, but failed to wear. One friend internalizes the dusting and calls the therapist she hasn't seen in two years. And though there is some effort in me to do as my friends do—to make room in my closet, to scour my psyche—I find quite the opposite occurs.

You would be as hard-pressed to find a farmer who is only a farmer as you would to find an artist who isn't subsidizing her creativity and career in some other way. Farmers in winter are carpenters or get requests to do some off-farm machinery repair, like actresses who work as cocktail waitresses for extra money. I am not yet sure if being a farmer and an artist is economically feasible for me, but I contend that my two jobs complement each other. Not that they are harmonious so much as they are like old friends, lovingly antagonistic, forcing each other to be honest and contemplative. I do not, in any case, believe one would be any good without the other.

There are moments in March when my clay pots, sculpture, unwired lamps and incomplete collages cry out for conclusion, when my writing contains the grit and froth of many ideas but no cohesion.

The closer I come to planting the first of my spinach, ideas and images swell in my mind, refusing to acknowledge time and its limitation. It is this very creative insistence that makes me run to the routine of dawn-to-dusk

work, no matter if it is only unloading fertilizer, or making and taking lunch to the field so the day's planting is
minimally interrupted by meals. I long for the obligatory
tasks that cannot be left undone and for the satisfaction
of knowing I have finished them. My writing always feels
as if something could be better said.

Farming is nearly, if not absolutely, the opposite of
creating prose or poetry. As a writer, one can expect long
spells of unproductivity, but such "spells" would mean the
end of a farmer. In agriculture, time to ponder is undesirable and resented, even treated with suspicion. Farming is
a literal cultivation that demands physical movement,
timely responses and grim determination.

While I may long to write or paint, I cannot ignore
the weaklings in the vegetable propagation trays. We
have a space in the basement, under the stairs—essentially a climate-controlled closet, a grow room. When I
open the door, I am greeted by the artificial haze of ul-
traviolet lights. The first planting of tomatoes has
sprouted. Among them, the feeble are easy to spot. They
are the ones that do not remove their "hats". The seed
has split open, a tap root has descended and a spindly,
light green shoot has emerged. But the seed case has not
relinquished its hold and thus keeps the first energy-
seeking leaves knotted inside. There will be, with each
successive planting, many more seedlings like these, and
they will all call me and beg for my assistance. With
careful fingers, I might pry the snug bonnets off. But this,
I must tell myself, is not my job. If they are not strong
enough to do it themselves, they are not strong enough

to keep. These plants have exhibited their first hesitation and therefore are likely to be more vulnerable to disease. If I let them live, they are a potential threat to the health of the other seedlings. I feel sorrow, even empathy, but the practical farmer in me tells me to uproot them *now*, while the woman who pities and picks the drowning flies out of the dishwater says *wait*.

My shoes begin to come home with mud on their soles. I have transplanting to do. The mechanical implements I struggle to more fully comprehend begin their steady whine. In high volume, they drown creativity out. And the artistic dalliances I maintained all winter are now silenced in an irrevocably cluttered room.

THE FIRST FLOURISHES OF SPRING are not the crocus, but last year's vegetables, the ones that did not make it out of winter storage. A crate of butternut squash is dimpled with powdery orange and blue spots. I throw them on the compost heap, where they roll off the top to settle like spilled baubles between the dead leaves and slatted wall. Potatoes shoveled from a corner where they froze are dark purple, velvety, yet have a rankness that keeps me from touching them. I handle the little sacks with delicacy, as if they were rotten eggs, explosive. I open the doors on both ends of the greenhouse and sweep out the remains of tomatoes—translucent papery shards of red and yellow. Of hygiene and spring cleaning, my mother read aloud, and I hear the words all day, "due to the accumulation of dust mites, living and dead, in just ten years a mattress doubles in weight."

June is named for the patron goddess of marriage and is a month much easier to celebrate than March, which is the month the Romans named for Mars, the god of war. Though formerly Mars had been the god of fruitfulness and agriculture, I can imagine the ancients had one too many late starts, gave up on farming and fell into fighting. Feeding ourselves and killing each other are two of man's most distinguishably perfected talents. It's little wonder we should witness them side by side in March, the month of slow but certain seasonal abdication.

Chilly nights, especially the windy ones that sometimes follow a warm day, make me think of March as a battle between two women—a mother and a daughter arguing from opposite sides of the bedroom door. It's a closely matched fight, for what the younger might have in strength, the mother matches with will and stamina. The daughter is trying to shut her mother out. With her hands pressed against the door, she stands, feet planted, legs apart, a lunge dug in. She trembles with the strain of resistance while her mother works on the other side. The older one employs both intimidation and spurts of supernatural strength. She drums with her fists and forearms until the door rattles on its hinges. She ceases, recoils and then slams her well-proportioned hip against the unlockable entrance. Sometimes a part of her gets through; the water buckets ice over, we have a frosty morning. Our early conversations ride on I-can-see-your-breath clouds. The fight will not end violently but eventually, because the mother gives in.

From where I sit at lunch, I can see several flocks of Canada geese amassing in the rye field south of the house. It's a big, wide-open field and the geese, presumably on their way back north, hold fly-in happy hours throughout the day. Its hard to imagine monogamy, much less ordered flight, in such quantities—and yet the birds seem to do it, perhaps better than any other common living creature.

For other, less committed animals or less capable ones, March with its bright cold days seems to offer some kind of hope. Gelded creatures turn spunky. Old ponies with sway backs are inspired to flirt. I watch one, his neck arched, his arthritic knees becoming high and graceful, making a damn good effort to be as defiant of gravity as the mythic Arabian stallions who live on camel's milk and dates. The mares who've been turned out in the adjacent pasture ignore his charade. They begin to graze, nibbling at the beginnings of new grass as the old pony trots maniacally back and forth along the fence line. He whinnies. In March, pipe dreams have their longest runs.

The cat on the kitchen table wakes up when sparrows land on the porch. She flicks her tail and makes a guttural, chattering noise. She watches the birds, thinking of the time she will spend later, when she will catch and eat them. She yawns and I see the width of her mouth. It makes me think of boa constrictors, which can unhook their jaws to swallow their victims. The cat curls up to sleep; this is how one hunter plots.

Later in the afternoon, when Jigger is showing me how to take apart and inspect the brakes of the new (to me) 1948, Super "C" tractor, I am listening and watching but still itching. I am thinking about beating the carpets, hauling my bed off its frame. I want to open all the doors and ask the old woman in for one more killing frost.

THE FIRST LOADS OF SEED POTATOES arrived on Friday. We won't start planting any earlier than the end of the month, or if the weather keeps up like this—cold and damp—not until the first, maybe second, week in April. Jimmy was halfway through unloading the tractor trailer when the rain turned to snow—large, messy clumps. Snow in March is as tormenting as it is absurd, like winter got its zipper stuck.

But we are consoled, we know it can't last. During coffee break we sit by the woodstove in the back of the shop looking out the open door. The snow hurls itself onto the oblivion of warmer pavement and earlier puddles. The icy squall will pass, and a scant, see-through blanket will persist only where the sun cannot reach. This is not to say Long Island can't play host to a spring blizzard. A morning like this, when we feel trapped in a seasonal holding pattern, is when someone brings up the eight inches that once fell on Easter Sunday. Most of the crop had been planted and a lot had even sprouted; farmers lost acres. Tales of woe generally start with the most recent account and then move back in history and up in severity. By the time we hit the 1930s, Dean has generally grown impatient or too anxious to hear more. He'll stand up, take his hat, and say, "Well, we're not getting anything done sitting around here."

A short time ago, I read an essay, "The Feathered Harbingers of Spring", written by Adelaide E. Topping near the turn of the nineteenth century. Her grandson, Alvin, has been careful to save the fragile letters, wedding invitations, birth announcements, and obituaries that span the several generations of his family, one of Sagaponack's oldest. The accumulation, Alvin assures me, is daunting, but as a collection, the news items, random as they may be, provide a local history. The accounts that were clipped and stashed in envelopes and then categorized in boxes that eventually filled the attic are the verbal fine points that the photograph has largely replaced.

Adelaide was originally from Quogue, a town about thirty minutes west of here. However, when she met and married Frank Topping, she was considered "from away", meaning it was at least a day's ride off. The house that she and her husband lived in still stands at the northeast corner of Gibson Lane, just across from the cemetery. The home was built for her as a wedding present.

Soon after she settled in, Adelaide, who was employed as a teacher at the Bridgehampton School, helped found the Sagaponack Literary Club. This group of men and women routinely convened to share and discuss works that its members had penned. For them, it seemed, these meetings were not just opportunities to pore over personal issues, gossip and drink tea, but more like expository writing classes. Each meeting was an occasion to educate each other on a specific topic of interest, which in most cases required independent research and observation. Adelaide's essay, written a few days after the vernal equinox, carefully and poetically considers the tiny birds that, along with the lengthier days, signaled spring to her. She writes about the homely and taken-for-granted sparrow with convincing appreciation.

> The whole family of Browns, or sparrows arrive. They are by every roadside, every thicket and stump-strewn pasture. Let us not think that every sparrow we see is the English sparrow. If we study this family of birds closely we will see the song sparrow, with converging streaks on its upper breast, the fox sparrow in a fox-brown mantle, the tree sparrow with a jet black pin across his breast, the field sparrow, vesper sparrow, swamp sparrow, chipping sparrow, white-throated sparrow, who are on their way to bring gladness into happy spring time.

Occasionally Adelaide mentions birds I have never heard of, and I assume this is because we've come to name them differently. For example, the purple grackle is called the "crow-blackbird". The woodpecker that she refers to as "golden winged", I believe, is our increasingly common northern or yellow-shafted flicker. The "crescent marked" and the "spotted breast," however, remain a mystery.

> The tiniest of these is the bluebird. We appreciate the first birds and the first flowers for they bring to life some glad consciousness that has lain dormant for the past four months.

Bluebirds are the first arrivals from the south, from Florida and way stations, they alight in our fields and pastures and gardens and herald the coming of the minstrel choirs. The males are the first to arrive, coming singly or in small straggling companies. When the females come a little later, the males are in full song, and the period of courtship, which is very ardent in bluebirds, begins.

When I read this, I read it three times; to see a bluebird in Sagg is an experience I could emphatically call rare. It is saddening to know but delightful to imagine that these songsters were once expected and customary with each new spring. In a separate later article from 1953, Ernest Clowes, the author of "Wayfarings" (a collection of columns that had appeared in the *Bridgehampton News*, 1941 to 1953), laments that a bluebird hadn't been seen in these parts for many years. But then, just last summer, I spotted a pair in Poxabogue cemetery and experienced something probably similar to the "glad joy" Adelaide mentioned. Her favorite birds have not deserted this neighborhood forever.

FROM FAR OFF I CAN SEE THE SEAGULLS, flying together like a slow-turning tornado. The gulls follow the plow because the earth it turns over is plentiful with whatever burrows down for the cold months—bugs, worms, grubs. When they've exhausted what the plow serves, the birds will shadow the planter, for it too stirs up ground and offers a second helping. After a winter of eating carrion, shellfish and deli lunch leftovers, the gulls find the grubs plump delicacies. Plus, here, in the field that abuts an ocean, the gulls have the advantage of proximity. As word of just-plowed ground makes it over the dune banks, the great blackbacks beat both the grackles and crows to the freshest meal in town. Today it looks to be mostly immature ground beetles. The seagulls are gracious vultures. They hover above as a flock but take turns; a few at a time drop down in the furrow. They walk with purpose, very upright and alert, businessman-like, to pluck the sleepy, unsuspecting larvae.

Now my world becomes small because we have one focus: to plant three hundred acres of potatoes. Weather depending, it will take about a month, a very long month. I watched my father, who has done this job so long you'd think he'd grow weary, drum the breakfast table with his hands. "It's time to stir up ground!" He says this with sincere, even impatient enthusiasm. My father is over six feet tall, but bent by two hip replacements, and it takes him a little longer to stand. Not this morning; he's out of the chair and heading for his coat; he is straight and limber. I selfishly wonder if his stamina has something to do with the fact that my brother and I grow increasingly committed to farming. Routines have developed, and we can work well together. I imagine that for my father, having grown children behind—or sometimes in front—of him, is as close as he'll ever come to acknowledging his own success.

However, this gung-ho atmosphere exists at 6:00 A.M., before anything but sunlight has been encountered and, in general, I know that Cliff's good mood is fragile and, therefore, often fleeting. The frailty of our relationships is most evident during planting. This is partially because we have a specific window of time. Tight schedules, be they created by bosses in suits or by limited growing seasons, tend to make people uptight. The second reason we're so vulnerable in spring is that on our farm, at this time of year, at least one piece of equipment comes out of the shop with modifications. It used to be my father who dreamed up hydraulic, labor-saving devices, but now Dean shares in the art, and where there was once master and apprentice, there are now two near-equals. Both of them are often so full of ideas and theories about how to achieve the ideal that it is easy and probably necessary for them to clash.

Improvements to equipment or entirely original pieces, the ones they invent are called "rigs". And in the spring, when these rigs make their headland début, we all stand around and wait to see how and if the new thing works. When Dean's rig fails, or when Cliff's is off-kilter, an exchange somewhere between I-told-you-so antagonism and genuine yet misconstrued desire to amend the problem fills the air. It is a rivalry, and though the words often get very ugly, I know that if my brother can survive this and still want to farm, I'll have a business partner for life. A family farm, though essentially a business, is first a family and has a tendency to behave like one. We all get yelled at and we all yell. Anger is displaced all the way down the proverbial totem pole, where at the end, one hopes the wrath will be so feeble that it gets shrugged off and forgotten, nearly.

Yesterday the *New York Times* ran a piece chronicling a woesome outlook for family farms in America. Although the article profiled family-owned ranches in Nebraska, it contained bits of relevance for small farms everywhere. Not only is there the emergence of corporate factory farms that grow so much and for so little (often because they have no conscience and are able to take advantage of cheaper labor and the environmental naiveté in poorer countries), but there have also been misspent subsidies and shortsighted legislation. At the very core of this dilemma is the American farmer, who has been continuously productive, perhaps too productive. In the end the nonfarming population expects cheaper and cheaper food and it makes very little difference what hemisphere, much less what state, it comes from. It is a simple but vicious cycle that if left to its own momentum, the author contends, will turn much of rural America into ghost towns.

Our potato crop is sold by the tractor trailer load to vegetable brokers in Puerto Rico. The price paid fluctuates with both regional supply and international demand. We know when it's raining in Delaware or snowing in Maine. We know when Prince Edward Island starts harvesting: our market goes through the floor and we don't move anything for two weeks. It is precarious and depressing. Conversely, I can also experience the other end of the American farm spectrum with my farm stand, where every tomato costs seventy-five cents, and even if the local supermarkets are selling Ecuadorian asparagus for $1.69, I can still sell mine for $3.50. And I don't sell it for twice the price just because I can, but because I pick every spear by hand, every day. Here, on the fertile outskirts of Manhattan, many farms, while no longer the basis for a thriving economy of potatoes or cucumbers, have been able to align themselves with a local fresh market. It is an ironic blessing that as trendy as this place becomes, and as overpriced and overcrowded, the part-time population wants not just its views but its tastes. Today, within a two-mile stretch of road, there are four farm stands on Sagg Main. Twenty years ago there was just one self-serve that sold mostly fall crops; Brussels sprouts, cabbage, ten-pound bags of potatoes. No matter what you are told, though celebrated for its agricultural conditions, Sagaponack does not count as part of rural America. A tumbleweed would not tumble along a deserted Main Street just because the farms folded. What is likely to happen to the little guys of Nebraska (being gobbled up by corporate entities) won't happen to us.

I take comfort in my farm stand, as if it is something, should potatoes become as unprofitable for us as they have for most of Long Island, that we could diversify further and make our living from. But I also frequently feel that selling fine produce to an elite sector of the population isn't exactly farming. And I suppose I am as guilty as the rest of the romantics who imagine farming as the noble, humble profession of feeding everyone, the poor as well as the rich.

APRIL HAS LIVED UP to and beyond its reputation. These are not gentle showers that collect in a daffodil's yellow folds. These are drenching, daylong downpours, ones that drive worms right out of the ground, only to drown them in the puddles. It is relentless rain that beats the color out of pansies.

Every other day of planting has been held up by the weather. There has been eight inches in just two weeks. Optimistically speaking, it is good that we are behind schedule. If we were on schedule, we'd be nearly done and then the entire crop, rather than a portion of it, would be sealed into the thoroughly soaked darkness, vulnerable to the diseases that thrive in such cold, wet conditions.

April is not a good time to cross a potato farmer; we're on edge, preoccupied; we're thinking of only one thing besides the weather and that's the planting. While it is a relief to be back in the field, it's also a little like running a race when you're out of shape; you know a finish line exists, but you're not sure what it will take to get there. It is not possible to predict all the personal, mechanical and environmental malfunctions. If the fertilizer truck should break down, or the motor on the seed conveyor burn out, everything grinds to a halt. You're likely to get stiff, winded and cranky. There is the added difficulty that planting doesn't depend on just one pair of legs, but six. Our perennial marathon feels like a convoluted version of the three-legged race, where all that is set in motion doesn't necessarily head in the same direction at the same time. There is the person, generally my father, who plows. Behind him is the planting tractor, which Jimmy, because he can start and hold a straight line from one end of the field to the other, always drives. Jigger, ironically the most accident-prone of our employees, stands on the back of the planter—a narrow steel shelf with a little seldom-used seat in the middle. It permits Jigger to see into the individual seed hoppers and make sure the seed is dropping correctly. Others who know Jigger, even in less pressing, slower-paced situations, like at the service station where he works on Sundays, would expect that with the way he gets his feet crossed up, we'd have trouble on the back of the planter. But Jigger has "ridden" the planter for countless other potato farmers, and for the past twelve years (we cross our fingers), without incident, he's done so for us.

The rest of us are stationed back at the farm. Norman and Slim cut seed. My brother is busy repairing, maintaining, coordinating, while I grease equipment, deliver loads of fuel and coffee. It sounds simple, but never is.

Last week as we planted, I was called to the field to haul debris out of the way. There were great sheets of plastic—the industrial-strength cellophane that wraps insulation, spackle buckets, coffee cups, lots and lots of cardboard. The stuff had blown in from the numerous and adjacent construction sites. I know there won't ever be a law banning building, but I'd be satisfied if they'd just implement a mandate for covered dumpsters. I have come to revere farming as an art form, and anything that sullies the landscape, our borrowed canvas, somehow and slowly erodes morale.

For those who see but don't partake in the steady progress we make across a field, planting may look easy. Even those who are intimately involved with the discipline are apt to call it cold, repetitious and mechanical. When I am caught up in planting and the pace at which we strive to do it, it is hard to see or admire the fact that the entire process is choreographed. The mishaps, once they're survived, are often remembered as brilliant bits of improvisation. A deer's broken antler punctures a tire, and within moments the jack, air compressor and manpower are there to fix it.

Like many arts, potato planting can be viewed purely for its visual impact. I've often tried to explain exactly what it is that makes this place more beautiful than others. Often and very casually, people will say that the quality of light out here on the East End of Long Island is different. While I don't disagree with tourist dogma, I am never satisfied with my own ability to understand why, and convincingly describe how, this sublime atmosphere occurs. It doesn't do to merely say that we have pink afternoons, gold mornings and fogs that stop both sound and movement. This is a fertile island, with not just open spaces growing different-colored crops, but with a certain, often negligible, dampness—suspended moisture that intensifies an object or a landscape by surrounding it.

I watch as the plow breaks winter's seal. There is the slightest sense of violence when I see the furrow it carves, the way six silver plowshares can mirror the sky as they cut into and lay over the land. For me, nothing is as truly green as our cover crop in spring. The rye comes back to life, beating the trees to leaf and the lawns to grass; it commands. Then the plow tears through this wavering sheet. It stills it, like a hand over a scream. And now that dirt—there is not in any artist's palette a burnt sienna more enviable than that of Sagaponack's black-flecked, iron-warmed soil—is earth that can hold you. As the plow makes its way across the field, turning one color into the other, it enables a contrast by which we recognize fecundity. Even people who have never set foot on a farm can watch that plow and honestly, quietly comment, "Wow, you've got nice ground here."

Potato planting is also a musical feat. The planter itself is like the symphony hall, an acoustic shell. Inside the planter are the countless moving parts, metal parts, and while "the Lockwood" is not half so pretty as the innards of a baby grand, there is a ringing combination of clacking sprockets, recoiling springs, the high-pitched thump of an empty seed hopper or the sudden thud of a shot bearing. If one is willing to listen, the planter provides a daylong concert of relationship between the seed and the soil. And when I see Jigger there on the back of the machine, I know that he has the unique position of being both the conductor and the dancer. One moment he is stepping lightly from one hopper to the next, but in the other, he hears something out of line and jabs a long oak stick to dislodge snared seed pieces. His baton flailing downward, directly Jigger realigns his orchestra.

A day of planting, even when I find myself occasionally, if not happily, distracted by the mastery of this art, is exhausting. The only time we rest is at lunch, a no-frills, fast picnic, where the idea of the perfect spot isn't a sunny hillside but rather tucked between trucks out of the wind. What begins as soon as sun comes up often lasts until it sets. We quit when there is just enough light to get home safely. And sometimes, just before the delirious shuffle back to the farm begins, we'll silently gather around the idling assortment of vehicles. These collective moments when nothing is moving and the mind holds a bleary focus over the fifteen newly planted acres are rare but familiar. Dirt is in our ears and gathered up at the hinge of our lips. Our eyes have caught dust all day. It's only now that I notice the discomfort of the small hard piles I've blinked into their edges. We're assessing and satisfied.

THE FIRST WEEK IN MAY took us from a snow shower to seventy degrees. A dandelion on the protected sunny side of the barn finished out its short life. The dogs raced past and one grazed the seed-filled halo to send a hundred silver needles spinning. Pesky and Ivy are the champions of euphoria. Shedding their winter coats, they answer to an airborne, blameless joy that seems to emanate from everywhere on days like this. The dogs indulge completely and unselfconsciously. Every possible smell of spring—grass stains to roadkill—is sampled, rolled in, and worn. They flaunt their smells and jump up into open laps to share. The weekend was pure bliss.

The white-throat sparrow is tireless in our backyard. It sits in the top of the blooming but sickly pear tree, going on and on with its call, which though likened to a lilting "oh, sweet Canada, Canada, Canada", seems much slower than that, and sadder too. The song is hollow and tapers off, as if the bird decides to give up to silence.

Nest building for humans is a ritualized process but is rarely so gracefully executed as it is with the birds. Flocks of people descend on racks of baby clothes. We hold gaudy "girl" parties that aren't nearly as fascinating as a pair of wrens, bearing nursery essentials, coming and going from their chosen spot.

At least three pairs have settled nearby. The males spend their day divided by chores and charisma. One returns with a twig, but also must swing by a convenient perch to remind the immediate world of his territory and intentions. Males are bold. Wrens are the type of birds that get right in the house cat's face for a good dressing-down. One sings from the tangle of multifloral rose beyond my neighbor's greenhouses, another answers back from the spires of bittersweet that have come to dominate the hedge. The pair I have been watching most closely is setting up in the old weigh house that stands on the edge of our property. The home they're making, though perfect in every other way, is in a hotly contested region of the yard. The forsythia is a favorite haunt for sparrows, and the common barnyard birds gather in mobs to bully the littler wrens. Fortunately they can do more than intimidate, for the wrens are the only birds that can actually make it inside the weigh house. A slit at the top of the door is no more than an inch or so wide and thus prohibitive to the menacing and already too abundant sparrow.

I get a stool to peer inside the high window of the weigh house. In an old newspaper box, still on its post, propped against the corner, the wrens have woven a deep nest. To the credit of the species, the wrens have a tidy home within a home. They are well out of predatory reaches; they have a nicely shingled roof and four solid walls.

Birds are thrifty and unconventional when it comes to housing. They all have preferences; barn swallows want mud, as do robins; flickers hollow nests out of trees; starlings prefer to squat and cowbirds just deposit their eggs in someone else's nursery, for someone else to raise. But generally birds use what's handy: the pieces of mane that horses snare and leave in the split rail, string, dog fur, dryer lint, candy bar wrappers and, of course, feathers—their own and those of others. This spring the sparrows have discovered "Elvis" and they are taking him, bit by bit, away for their needs.

Elvis is the scarecrow I built to protect my strawberry patch. Originally he was the younger Elvis replete with sequins, mirror glasses and stylish ebony wig. But his head, not unlike those of other scarecrows, is just a pantyhose—shaped and stitched and stuffed with a soft, spun-nylon fiberfill. Elvis once had a smug, commanding appeal out there in the berries, not a frumpy farmhand but instead the rock star of stars. The sparrows, though, apparently found a weak spot in the aging icon's chin and from it they have emptied the stuffing and much of the King's self-satisfied expression.

This spring, Elvis looks to be heavily into the downers. His wig has slipped lower, and now looks plastered, more dubiously unkempt, to his brow. The mirror shades have slipped partway down his nose and hang cockeyed in the stolen cheek's void.

At dusk, down nearer the swamp, another spring ritual takes to the air. To the unfamiliar ear, the noise is reminiscent of a loose fan belt—a high-pitched wavering. But the sound is from tree-clinging, soprano amphibians, the *Hyla crucifer*, or as it's most commonly called, the "peeper". The "peep" is a mating call.

To catch and hold a peeper, you have to cup it within a gentle fist. The hand is barely sensitive enough to feel the cool body as it probes between fingers looking for an out. As I open my hand, which I eventually must, the peeper doesn't leap or flinch or in any other way struggle to escape. I hold this tiny thing—no bigger than a large housefly—up for closer inspection. I press my fingertip to its delicately heaving side, against its nearly transparent skin, touch the cross mark that gives the frog its name. Little else so loud and alive has a skeleton like this, sharp and complicated, shifting under a loose-fitting covering. Such an intricate thing, such a miniature heart.

I do not understand, but I recognize the mythic chemistry between humans and frogs. How else can we explain the frog prince who, with one kiss, becomes the man capable of answering a woman's dreams? I do not know if the tale is an allegory about the nature of men or the power of a kiss, but I open my windows at night to hear the peepers. And the longer I listen, the better I become at recognizing the individual princes—the different pitches and tempos that penetrate the silence to combine as one, like the first note of an orchestral composition. Tonight, I can hear the prince playing the piccolo's part.

LAST YEAR WE BEGAN CUTTING ASPARAGUS on the first Friday in May, and I picked vegetables every day from then on until the first of November. We are now just two weeks into asparagus season. When we go out to cut, the first thing I notice is how dry, even in early morning, the field is. Wind witches, miniature tornadoes of dust, rise up, come straight for us, but then, as if they've gotten a closer look and changed their mind, veer off to the south and disappear over the potato field.

A whole lot of nothing is what it is. Squall lines from which we expect rain gather clouds, but nothing more. They die out dry as dry. It hasn't rained, or at least nothing memorable, in nearly a month. It is the *pump, pump, pump, tsk, tsk, tsk* of the lawn sprinkler that keeps the azalea and the bleeding heart alive. My lettuce looks like it dies every day. It wilts—flat, lifeless. I drag out my irrigation pipe and the lettuce, forgiving, comes back resilient at night. I ask Cliff how long until we have to water the potatoes. "I don't know," he says. "Soon." I can tell he's irritated that I needlessly remind him.

Becoming a farmer has been a gradual immersion, not a baptismal dunk. Learning is a slow, deliberate process, something like wading into the Atlantic for the first swim of the year. The cold cuts me off at the ankles;

then, as the water splashes behind my knees, I am halved at the waist. The iciness is only a threat now to the parts the water hasn't touched; it teases what's left to go under. I hold my arms up as if to protect my armpits against the agony. Like the ocean's chill, my never-ending farm lessons are exhilarating. No two days, no two years of farming are ever the same. Sometimes, as with the frigid ocean, it is better to be out of it, recalling, rather than contending.

A simple concept of farming, primarily because it's an economic one, is *the earlier the better*. And of roadside stands this is especially true. If you are the first with vine-ripe, quality tomatoes, you have the coveted prize that people have been waiting eight months for. I shall never be the first with tomatoes because the varieties I grow are called "heirlooms" and they've never been hybridized to ripen early. I tolerate their slow-growing attribute only because I believe their looks and flavor to be superior to the regular red tomato. However, merely because I accept the consequences of heirloom traits doesn't mean I sit back patiently. I, like most other farmers, try to coax, even fool, the plants into believing it's summer well before it is.

This year the heat made transplanting the tomatoes a sort of damned-if-you-do-or-don't procedure. On one hand, the heirlooms are old enough to be out of the greenhouse and in the ground. But on the other, and perhaps more important, hand, the environment I prepared for them, with all its heat-keeping properties, could cook the young plants. First, I stretch and tuck row after row of black plastic mulch into the dirt. In cooler weather, the mulch serves to preheat and then hold the heat overnight. And then there also is the row cover, a white cocoonlike cloth that forms a gossamer but effective tunnel over each row. It's as if I have a mile-long, miniature greenhouse. Faced with a heat wave, I am unsure. Should I tear up the mulch? Should I lift off the tunnels, those scalding chambers? Yet, to do so is to expose my heirlooms at night and, like my sunburned arms, they'd be doubly chilled.

Because I am far from the likes of my father, or even my brother, I have yet to acquire in my bones a sense of when it is time to plow, or plant, or when it will freeze or frost or rain. I keep a written record of when it does.

A weather journal is an easy diary to keep; it requires no internal debate, nor does it map mood swings, failures or heartaches. Despite this, emotions are not altogether excluded from my meteorological reverie. As I page through last year's entries and read, "rain . . . rained 2" in two hrs . . . still raining . . . stopped but too wet to plant . . . rained at night", a feeling of powerlessness is rekindled. I never want to live through a spring as wet as that again. Reading on brings back a lucid image of potato seed-pieces afloat in the lakes that had been our fields. I remember with disgust what I saw when the water finally receded: all of it, the seed, lying in a line like debris left at the high tide mark. Our projects and labor seemed to be lying there too. Last year was so different; it is hard to believe I am still writing from the same region. Not unlike the bad poetry I'll find someday, secreted away in a little locked book, that will hardly represent the emotionally detached realist I've become.

I abbreviate and record things like temperature, quality of sunlight, the precipitous and culminating events—the day we started planting potatoes, with a star; in red ink are the mornings we had frost, underlined six times is the date of the last frost. I note the blackbird's return and the junco's departure. I have yet to decide if this journal will make me a better farmer. Though I may write it all down, year after year, all I ever have is a record of what's history. Does this better my odds of prediction? Will I ever see a bad spring coming? Or will I just have skimpy literary notes to bring up the past, the sometimes unpleasant past, and thus learn to fear all seasons? For the climate always seems to be on the verge, like now, of being too dry. And then it is too hot, too wet, too cold. As changeable and as intemperate and as inconsiderate of my needs the weather may prove to be, there is this prevailing fact that all the same, I must rely on it. In the terminology of romance, I have to believe the season will always work out, if only in the way a shotgun wedding does.

MY FATHER LOOKS UP FROM THE NEWSPAPER, lets out a blasé laugh—one syllable that registers between "ha" and "ugh". He muses quietly, under his breath but not necessarily to himself, "Memorial Day. That's when all the people show up—it's also about the same time I start seeing potato beetles. I don't know which is the worst pest."

Not all families grow old eating breakfast together. And I am not sure I'd wish it on others, but for now, the time the four of us spend eating toast, complaining that it's burnt, throwing the terriers biscuits, is a routine of function and convenience. Our conversation is a rough sketch for the day—who will do what and in what order. This means breakfast is also when we find out what hasn't, but should have, been done the day, week, or year before. It is when wits are taut but not necessarily right, and it gives rise to the worst disagreements, irrational escalations that end in finger-pointing. The entire room explodes. Dean and I move for a door; my mother goes to the sink; my father puts his shoes on in fuming silence. But breakfast has the potential for harmony too. The day may begin as peacefully as if we all ate alone. Fortunately, today will be like that.

In the past four years we've been through as many toasters. The latest incarnation of automatic breakfast ease needs to be watched. We don't take responsibility for each other's bread. Dean, who is behind the counter watching his toast, responds to our father's observation with a story, one that illustrates his point.

"You want to hear what happened to me?" And of course we do, because Dean always seems to witness the best things—from a bicycle blowing off the roof rack to an irate fiancée throwing her ring into the rye field—all from the cab of his tractor. We wait for his toast to finish. He comes to the table, smiling, but the grin has an edge, one that is somewhat bitterly amused.

He said it happened midday Saturday. Planting was going smoothly. The gusty wind that had made the earlier part of the week so provoking had finally let up. It was a beautiful day, in fact one of the few truly beautiful ones we've had this spring. It was not the kind of day a farmer would find himself easily irritated. Dean was prepping the ground for corn with the chisel plow. The chisel plow, unlike the mull board plow, "stirs" the ground. Twelve curved shanks cut through the ground, simultaneously breaking up hardpan and mulching in organic debris, and it takes a big tractor to pull it. So Dean, who has an affinity for big and powerful tractors, was happy to be driving the largest one he owns—a Case Stieger, 350 horses under its hood. All eight of its tires are the same size, over six feet tall. It's one of the few tractors that is both fun and easy to drive down our crowded summer streets. Cars, though they could probably fit underneath, hastily give way. But not only is this tractor formidable. If driven correctly, it can maneuver in incongruously tight areas and leave the land as neat as any tractor can.

As Dean worked his way toward the west side of the field, he could see that the residents of a bordering house had thrown much of their spring cleanup over the low hedge and into the field. It's not uncommon to find this sort of thing, or worse, a swimming pool drained into the fields. On a bad day, the refuse would have provoked, even insulted, Dean, but today he was content with a tit-for-tat statement. Be it lost dogs or dead branches, you should return to people what is rightfully theirs. When the pruned branches were in his path, he simply climbed out of the tractor and heaved the branches, one by one, back over the hedge. He returned to the tractor, had bumped the throttle up a notch, when a small, angry eight-year-old stormed onto the field.

It used to be that kids were in awe of tractors. They used to play in sandboxes pretending any and every toy was a tractor, if in sound only—jaw clenched, lips sputtering, *bbbrum, brum*, each exhale a new exertion, a more powerful gear. The boy confronting Dean was standing on the edge of the lot and gesturing angrily. The words he chose couldn't be heard above the tractor's engine but his rage was exhibited in his posture. His squinting expression, neck extended, his adamant fist telling the farmer just where to go. The eight-year-old appeared to not only want to take on Dean but the tractor too. Though piqued by the child's intensity, Dean chose to ignore the Clint Eastwood prodigy. But then the confrontation escalated to a new level.

The child went back to the other side of the hedge to an arsenal of stacked wood and commenced to hurl next winter's heat into the field. Dean stopped and this time shut off his tractor. The boy, perhaps now comprehending the magnitude of his offense, vanished.

As Dean got out of the tractor, an older man sheepishly made his way into the field. As the father began to pick up the logs, he hollered back to his naughty, out-of-sight offspring, "Young man, did you throw these sticks out here? You can't do that! Get out here and help me clean this up!" The child now peeked from behind a row of cedar trees and shook his head defiantly, refusing to venture back into the field. He shouted back his improbable defense, "I did not. I didn't do it."

By now Dean's good mood was wrung out. The situation, the bold-faced lie and the cowed father picking up after his bratty son, seemed to embody everything that was wrong with the world. Dean approached and leveled, "Yes sir, he DID do it." He checked his irritation, wanting it exposed but not explosive, "but that's okay, kids tend to cut up." Then with a little less restraint, to break even, Dean added, "But I'll tell you what," and he gestured toward the silent, now tearful assailant, "that kid needs a severe ass-warming." The father blanched and stumbled through an unlikely explanation, "Well . . . well, his ass is still warm from last night!"

MEMORIAL DAY, here again and there is no stopping it. We all need the summer, though in different incarnations. As potato farmers we need the warmth and long days. Others need people buying T-shirts, sandwiches and tickets to charity benefits. It used to be I had a harder time with the seasonal loss of territory, but now I find myself more distracted or concerned by matters other than overcrowding at the post office. All the potatoes are up but it hasn't rained since they were planted. They've found their moisture in the way the seed is set in small mechanically created hills. Dry as it is, you can dig into these ridges and find damp dirt still hiding there, letting the potatoes grow. For the spinach, beets and peas planted much closer to the surface, germination and growth are a little less certain.

PART OF BEING YOUNG AND FEARLESS on a farm was taking advantage of its architecture. A huge, rickety barn with crumbling lean-tos that once occupied most of our back-yard was a logical and unsupervised destination. The exterior of this building was unimpressive, covered mostly by mossy shingles that the horses, when bored, gnawed on. But inside were lofts, trap doors and cavernous spaces where things were stored and forgotten.

The years that the barn was used to store hay or straw were probably, in terms of terrain, the best. Harvesting straw, hoisting bales that weighed nearly as much as we did onto wagons, and then again by human chain unloading and restacking them in the mow—two bales this way, two that—was the hardest and scratchiest work I have ever known. When the barn was full, I couldn't tell if the tinderbox of straw we'd built inside actually helped hold up the oldest and most decrepit wing of the post-and-beam building. If I stood back near the fence, it seemed as if the windowless sides bowed more now than when we had begun. We wondered about the pile and if it should shift, could the whole thing, straw and timber, slide sideways and tumble down as one great heap into the front pasture? And yet, acknowledging the precariousness of the arrangement, we could not resist the wall of slippery gold bales.

As we climbed, we knotted our fingers through the sisal twine and wedged our toes between the bales. When strings let go, which they often did, the bale with one side loose responded to the uneven binding by letting its individual "flakes" jettison out of the elaborate, interlocking pile. I felt the snap, pulled my body tight to the "face" and froze. Other climbers, above and below, breathlessly waited for a slow schism, a restructuring tremor, to move through the entire mow. I resumed my climb then, a little less hastily.

At the top you were at eye level with the barn rafters. Someone had thrown, at some fortuitous moment, a rope up over the highest beam. It must have come off a whaling ship, and it was all small hands could do to get around the cable's girth, so a loop had been made, a single stirrup on which a bare foot would lead the whole body out over the canyon, an adjacent bay of broken and discarded bales. We took turns all afternoon, swinging, yet aware of the slow creak in the timbers that our small bodies triggered. Somehow, no rafter ever gave way.

There are other buildings on the farm that provided us with accessible rooftops. Because of the way potato cellars are built—into the ground—a shingled roof of forty-five degrees serves as a natural extension of the steep grass slopes that envelop and keep the storage barns cool. We did not entertain any danger by clambering up these roofs; we were light and the momentum of an error rarely carried us far.

Tonight, with my heavier and presumably easier-to-break body, I nearly talk myself out of trying to clamber up the potato cellar roof. I put my hands on the first course of shingles, press my palms down, then slowly drag them back. I am reminded of how my skin has an affinity for this grit: it knows and trusts the subtle traction. And though I won't scurry up on all fours, there are other postures, less vulnerable to gravity, that will get me there.

The nature of the longest days is that so much can fit into them that they have a way of seeming, conversely, the shortest. The potato field behind the farm only came into full blossom yesterday, but from up here on the potato cellar roof, the lifespan of the little white flowers is seen already rushing downhill. So much is possible in one of these days that the changes exhibited on the other side of short nights are drastic and obvious. Growth declines as quickly as it comes. And I can survey the changes from my vantage point.

The virtue of unnatural height comes in two opposing conceptions. One is a sense of purpose and control: royalty on a balcony overlooking the throngs. Or that of utter divorce: a loner in her high roost gazing down into a bustle she cannot significantly alter. One position affords the individual gumption or inspiration, while the other remains fast to the conventions of humility.

With my feet apart, I have gained a secure purchase on either side of the roof's peak. I can stand up straight, cross my arms and feel confidently anchored to this building. I can lean and rock. Nobody suspects I am here. People pass on bikes; their conversations are mine to pry. Birds fly below me. There are no mosquitoes. It is only my tomato patch in the foreground that disturbs this sovereign moment. The field, in the most ominous fashion, is showing me the detriment of excessive moisture. The foliage comes too quickly and worrisome imperfections show up in one of the weaker varieties. Here on the roof mulling over fungicides and prayers, it all seems more than a little beyond my reach.

FOR MUCH OF WHAT WAS LAST WEEK, Sagg did not exist. In the way some people have large but elegant noses, fog is a Sagaponack feature. Though imperfect, no other trait would satisfy. A fog sat down on us and pressed our tiny community into strange obliqueness. It is a frequent phenomenon here because we are surrounded by water. Our large, open tracts of land act as heat exchangers between day and night. We get that special condensation that lingers. You could not see someone if she passed you at arm's length. Footsteps draw invisibly closer and then when almost to you step suddenly further off. A woman buying asparagus calls it liquid air. At night or in early morning, the fog is luminous, making ghostlike slopes onto roads, out of pastures.

We grumbled some, worried playfully that the sun would never return. We could not help but marvel at the spiderwebs in early morning, hanging on tractor hitches, behind tires, on porch rungs, exaggerated by the moisture. Dampness gathered on my eyelashes and I thought of myself as a dewy mare left out for the night. In dense fog you can imagine yourself to be almost anything.

As vaguely predicted, the sun eventually came out and the fog lifted. Slowly, silently, the giant curtain of mist hoisted itself up into a rigged ceiling; now the colorful backdrop, the spring that had been obscured, brightened.

The wind brought down pear blossoms and the broken flowers landed on the porch like unmelted snow. White petals stuck to the dog's nose; the cats padded them into the kitchen on the bottoms of their paws. On my human feet, I tracked mud. Packed between the treads of my work shoes, it dried and broke loose on the terracotta tiles.

When I went out to transplant lettuce, the ground was technically still a little too wet to be worked. Though tilled up, it was on the heavy, waterlogged side and I fought with the incorrigible, rebounding rye that had been planted as a cover crop last October. I knelt and sank in. For a while, because I was pressed for time, I tried to streamline my transplanting effort. I worked like a robot, snatching two lettuce seedlings up, pivoting and swinging down in a single, awkward motion, gauging with my hands eight inches, then plunging the lettuce into the dirt. Efficient though I may have been, my attempt to automate the task from something I could daydream my way through into the tedium of focused repetition was counterproductive. When I straightened up to assess my progress, I found that my rows hooked and wove unsatisfactorily. I let the robot in me die. It was then that I noticed that the sun had brought the damp earth to the perfect temperature and I was within a cloud. My arms dragged voids of fog.

I watched as the asparagus patch, a hundred yards away, was overcome by the same effect. The soil's moisture had been heated and now rose into the cooler after-noon air. A thick mist formed and, to make it even more spectacular, the evanescence of the receding light turned the fog from white to blue to pink.

OUR EYES ARE FOR SEEING; they register proofs of our ex-periences that have no ready equations. Sagg Pond went out and now, reduced to a gunmetal gray slick, the only evidence of water is the birds that normally swim there. The swans run aground; an osprey hangs aloft but does not dive, in fear of breaking its neck; the sandpipers and plovers drill the mud. I watch through binoculars as a tern makes a circuit out over the ocean, where the glint takes it in and out of existence. It sweeps in low, across the pond's cut. Now the trees beyond, on Bridgehamp-ton's side, mark like picture frames the conclusion of the dropping flight.

The low pond puts the snapping turtles close to the surface. From Deacon's Island, I count the rectangular heads surrounding me—at a distance, but perhaps sniffing my flesh. And because I was once involved with hunting these prehistoric beasts, convinced that the wrong they visited upon ducklings justified my hoisting them from the muck, I also must consider possible vendettas. One turtle is the size of a sow. Just when you think the entire body has emerged, the neck extends again and more of its rugged shell pokes out of the dark water. I am rapt as it hauls itself onto the shore. Its armored body shines, and I see that the ancient, mossy ridge throws sunlight right back into the star's burning face.

My enchantment with the pond is constrained by the homes now built too close to it. The fundamental seasonal increase or decrease of the water level is tampered with according to the cellars, driveways and roads that are affected by high water. When complaints about flooding come rushing in, the town trustees and the Department of Environmental Conservation are enlisted to do something; they open the pond at its southern boundary so that it empties into the ocean, and the flooding is brought under control until the cut fills in and the pond begins to rise again.

What lurks here is a contradiction between alleged appreciation for the natural and a mandate by which we humans, for largely selfish reasons, strive to control our environment. It's no revelation; human self-interest disrupts not just this local ecosystem but global ones as well. However, there are days when Sagg Pond, with its come-and-go atmosphere—its radiance, then its quieting half-light—shows us the sublime. A small place persisting.

Summer

FLEDGLINGS ARE OUT in uncertain force. A catbird coaches hers into the top of the pear tree and then abandons them, giving the little ones no choice but to follow. Cromer the cat deposits battered tail feathers on the front stoop. A redwing blackbird is under the hedge thrashing something fluffy with his beak. I pull over and stop the larger bird from attacking the adolescent chickadee. Learning to fly, as a right of passage, is as mixed with danger as it is with delight. Birds have it hard. Almost everything eats them; we do, they do, pigs do, dogs, cats and turtles do.

I watch ladybugs feeding on clusters of freshly hatched aphids. In the morning fog, guinea hens canvas the asparagus patch, thirty birds to 3.5 acres, and they keep it nearly pest-free. Everywhere I look I see things eating each other, gathering the energy they'll need for the most important task of all. Consumption is an integral part of multiplication, and this is the most hospitable time of the year to raise young. We humans consider ourselves at the top of the food chain and our food supply so stable that we should be exempt from such territorialism and kingdom building, but this perspective is not altogether accurate. When hot weather has us rolling up our sleeves, we invite mosquitoes to dine. I think it is best to consider the food chain as the kind of chain that's got a clasp.

There are so many insects we could compare ourselves to. Sometimes we're squandering grasshoppers; other times we are like the industrious ants that swarm on the peonies today. They're not eating the flowers; instead they traipse around the tightly wrapped buds gathering nectar. I never thought of this before, but the ants work like nature's letter openers. The peony has yet to bloom. Its outer petals are stretched to near transparency and it is here, where the delicate wrappers overlap, that nectar seeps. Though I could find no source to prove a theory of symbiosis, it appears that when the ants gather the easily available nectar, they become greedy. They probe underneath the petals and thus their tiny but insistent prying helps to further loosen the flower's waxy bud and cause it to open.

Some ants are intentional agriculturists. The leaf cutters saw off bits of plants and carry the pieces back home. They arrange the clippings in special rooms where, as the leaf matter breaks down, mushrooms grow. It is on these mushrooms that the colony survives.

There are ants that keep "livestock", like dairymen. Sometimes they go so far as to erect leafy huts that corral their aphid cows for "milking". The aphid lives by sucking nutrients out of plants, and with its voracious appetite it produces a sizable, high-sugar by-product. Ants cluster around the aphids and, using their front legs, they stroke the aphid's abdomen. The aphid then excretes droplets of this "milk". In winter, these ants sometimes bring their "cow" with them deep down into the ground, out of the cold that would otherwise kill it. Since the aphid is no longer feeding itself, it no longer provides honeydew to the ants and so the hospitable act on the part of the ants appears to be compassionate. In reality, however, these ants are preplanning their first spring picnic. When the first seeds sprout, they carry their cow to the shoots and place her on it so she may feed at her leisure. The act of wintering over with the cow averts the hassle of shopping for a new milk giver in tight times.

Perhaps the most disturbing thing ants do for food is use each other as literal, living larders. When food is plentiful almost all of the colony works to collect it, but a few remain indoors to *just* eat. They consume load after load of plant nectars. They are eventually too fat to move and so they attach themselves to the ceiling and keep on eating. They spend their entire life in this service—as storage for their fellows and, when times grow lean, as redistribution centers.

I know and have experienced ants as pests. The carpenter ants that drop from the office ceiling and onto the typewriter startle me. But ants, like humans, have come up with reliable ways to attain and provide food, on one level doing very much what I do. Of course the majority of them participate in gathering food, whereas in this human colony we call America, only 2 percent of the population provides for the rest.

I PUT MY HANDS UP as both blinders and frame to exclude the architectural eruptions while establishing a long view of the field. I narrow my hands until I have just a corridor of different greens. I see one hue where the beets are coming on and another as the peas fill with flowers. The potatoes are nearly black as they meet the edge of the rye. The grain, as it moves in the wind, is either filled or emptied of light. The push is olive-gray and the rebound, when the sun is all caught up in the spiky awn, nearly gold.

It is the weekend we all know Sagaponack is capable of—the one weekenders have been waiting for. Strawberries are ready, and though they may need some sun and drought to sweeten, their cores have never been refrigerated. And this is the worthwhile difference.

The multifloral rose is blooming. I step out of the house and there it is, taking up all the air. Unlike so many other fragrances—daffodils, lilacs and even ocean breezes—multifloral is nothing to make a perfume of. It would not translate on human flesh; we'd smell overripe and cloying.

Most scents of our summer, if they could be packaged, wouldn't sell. Hot pavement might work, but only briefly, a sentimental novelty, reminding us of when we had the time and volition to spend an afternoon popping tar bubbles with our toes. Or horses: on warm damp mornings, their stalls take to the air. There is something familiar and welcoming in the acrid musk. Those who have pressed their noses to a sweaty horse's neck, and thankfully drawn the essence of control and authority into their systems, know that this lathered pungency, though cherished, could not sell, not even as an aftershave.

For a long time it was safe to sleep without the window screens, but nothing brings the insects out faster than a hot day in June. They, like us, at the first promise of an irreversible heat, flourish, eat and procreate. The June bugs drive themselves into the sliding glass doors. They masochistically assault the porch light. My cat, Airport, hunts them and in the morning when I go to feed her I see that my studio floor is littered with their spent carcasses. It is their wings that fascinate her. She rends the delicate sinews with her incisors as if she could unfold their secret organs.

Flea beetles materialize out of still soil. They come in droves to snip perfectly round holes in the cleome. They make lace of the arugula. One way to kill them is to walk and clap your hands as you go, just above the vegetation. Because the flea beetle is a jumper like its namesake, you'll get a few.

It was not until we had an acre of asparagus that I saw the asparagus beetle. And when I caught one, I was enamored with its good looks—red, white and oil-slick blue. Distracted by its beauty, I erroneously guessed it both good and exotic. But when I held it up for my mother to see, she replied with contempt, not for my naïveté but for my fate, "That, my dear, is an asparagus beetle. You'll have lots of them." And I soon did. I also have spotted cucumber beetles, striped cucumber beetles, aphids in every color, praying mantis posing as sticks in the raspberries and a bean beetle that, in its larval stage, looks exactly like very small star fruit. "Plant it and they will come" is my motto.

The Colorado potato beetle is well-known in Sagaponack. They used to plug up the neighboring pool filtration systems. At harvesttime their gaily striped exoskeletons stampeded across Daniel's Road, from the dug to the undug field. It was enough to make you skid off your bike. Hoards of these beetles would earnestly, inexplicably, scale the exteriors of houses. But the potato beetle at present doesn't pose the threat it used to, not here anyway, partially because there are fewer farmers growing potatoes on Long Island. While it feels good to be able to say that the bugs have lost their critical mass, that they don't have enough acreage to make living here worthwhile, ironically, many farmers admit this is also happening to them.

The year I first raised eggplant, I thought that my garden would single-handedly resuscitate the CPB (Colorado potato beetle) population. The bugs did something I thought to be very disconcerting, besides decimating the eggplant itself. They ate every part of the plant, every tender shoot and leaf; they scalped the vegetable of its foliage. And when there was nothing left to eat, the female glued her egg mass to the edge of a woody stem, as if she almost forgot. Potato beetles do not hatch with legs; they are little helpless slugs that dry up and die if they get too dusty. I wonder at a creature that, like ourselves, eats everything up and then pushes its progeny into a depleted environment.

Then there are the insects I like—bees and butterflies, dung beetles and ladybugs. The bees not only "share" honey, the food of gods, with us, but they do an incredible side job of pollinating. And just as butterflies are beautiful, dung beetles are comical—as if they have just found the most useful treasure in the world, they roll a piece of manure down the barn aisle.

Ladybugs have become agricultural mercenaries. Once it was discovered that they could themselves be "farmed" and that they could also survive a first-class trip in the mail, garden supply companies began peddling the not-so-dainty insect. I have a friend who released 850,000 ladybugs to take care of her pest problems. When it comes to appetite for other insects' larvae, her name is misleading. The ladybug is a voracious carnivore, especially when immature, when it looks and almost behaves like a very small, six-legged alligator, gray with just the slightest hint of pink in the middle of its long back.

As more farmers and homeowners turn to these and other beneficial insects for help, it is important to familiarize ourselves with their looks. It is so easy to impulsively swat the tickle in your hair or smush the many-legged monster that darts from the wood pile. But these creatures often exist as a means of controlling each other's population. And though we might not readily want to admit it, bugs—at least originally—played a very large part in keeping the human population in check. They are small enough to infiltrate and if left unchecked, prolific enough to devastate. If it weren't for those that eat each other on the way to the top, the top would probably have six legs, not two.

A FEW DAYS AGO I got a letter from a friend: "Asparagus gone already . . . and spinach too? Soon it will be berries and then tomatoes. And then it will be winter again." It is philosophically claimed that the speed of life increases when all is well. If it were thus, we'd create rapid chapters of easy times. The long, drawn-out dissertations remain for the not-so-easy. Besides the fast and the slow passage of time, there is that time that stands still, when you are waiting but are not yet impatient.

Here in Sagaponack, we are just beginning, not anxious yet, to wait for rain. The way the season has been so far—taking us to the brink of dehydration, then damn near drowning us, then another dry-out spell—it has been a good growing year. Tonight when I look from the bed of my truck at the sunset and the way it complements my garden, I cannot help but wonder if our lush good luck is not over. I fret a little; to have the heavenly spigot turn off would break my heart.

The string beans are almost in flower. To check their progress I needn't stop walking; I can reach down and let my hand trail through the canopy. Leaves lift and fall back, hesitating partway down, like the cover of a new book. There I feel the slightest patter—tightly folded, swaddled flowers as they bump against each other. Right now a gentle half inch of rain, one that takes the whole day, would open the flowers up to bees and wind and incidental pollination.

The peas, their harvest now in full swing, bear testimony to the kind of spring we had. One of the earliest crops, they have taken advantage of the spring-like-spring-ought-to-be weather. I have never had peas like this: rows bending to rows with knee-high corridors, and from tangled buttresses the endless decor of dangling, waxy pods. They are enchanted garden peas, storybook peas, thousands of peas.

When picking, determined as I might be, I seldom make it to the far end of the row. Usually when I look at this kind of abundance I feel frantic: I must pick and sell it all. But maybe because this crop is peas, and if I were to disc them down tomorrow, they'd put enough back nutritionally to make the crop worthwhile, I don't feel as desperate as I would if it were raspberries or tomatoes. Besides, I know the birds have found the peas, and the time I can pull them easily by the fistful will end.

In past seasons I've been either stingy or unrealistic, never planting enough peas for me *and* the grackles. Once the birds know where the peas are, unless I can stand guard from twilight on, it's as good as over for my harvest. Birds line the fence and fill the trees waiting for me to leave the field. A redwing blackbird perches on the snow pea trellis and calls it his own. Some birds batter the shells with their beak until they can pull the peas through the tears, but not grackles. Grackles amble like window shoppers, so distracted by the goodies that they ignore my clapping hands. One pauses, glances back over its oily shoulder, assessing the distance between us. Then, defiantly it strikes a long green pod. It hits what must be a spring-loaded trigger and eight peas are instantly exposed.

For all my fingers, I am not as adept as the grackle, but I practice what I imagine is a slick, single-handed motion of pulling, shelling and eating the pea. A gentle squeeze and then a minuscule pop. The pod in my hand is now invitingly ajar . . . for a thumb to rattle up its spine, to snap the thread that holds the perfect pea.

AS THE EARLIEST CROPS PEAK, any protest of their imminent passing is muted by the ease with which they are replaced. And this year, perhaps because I am becoming a more coordinated farmer, or more likely because my garden has had the benefit of accommodating, even inspirational, weather, I feel prepared.

Tonight I am especially thrilled with the tomatoes. They pulled out of the last soaking slowly but now have what looks like a healthy thirst, their vines reaching for everything. I use wire cages to protect these tomatoes from disease. They keep the plants upright and off the ground. Like this, the sun can reach in and the air can move around. And when the time comes, the cages also make the fruits easier to find. Tonight, the cages give the tomato patch a look that is more decadent than I am used to. Though they won't be able to do so for much longer, the cages are still capable of supporting the wild tangle of indeterminate vines. Each plant is threaded up and then evenly cascades out of the cage's three circular tiers. With the sun nearly down, the bright yellow blossoms are individual points of light. I know that because I am not yet hauling irrigation pipe. I have this leisure, this luxury, to sit watching the field as evening takes over and to think of these nightshade plants as exquisite chandeliers.

But when the sun finally sinks out of its cloudless sky, I grow uneasy. There's no setting, just a dusk taking over, glowing lavender until ten, stealing light from the stars. A sky like that doesn't give me much hope—not a drop of moisture in it. The time I now have for watching things unfold at their own, comfortable pace will be forfeited to hauling pipe for irrigation.

The potato that wants a drink kind of shrinks. Already in the fields, where there are patches of light or sandy soil, the stressed plants stick out. There are isolated areas of darker foliage and mean-looking, rolled leaves. I was concerned to hear that scientists had installed a jellyfish gene in the potato. The invented plant is meant only to be a nonedible moisture marker; when it needs water, it glows. It worried me because I think a farmer should be able to look at any plant and scratch the dirt with her toe to tell when a potato needs watering. It's no great skill, just the most basic desire to understand rather than be told. It takes a few seasons of watching to know that when peppers need water they become too light a shade of green. Corn "pineapples." It stops growing, pales and seems to wind all its energy back in. In prolonged drought entire fields spike into the sky. Greens lie flat, as if they have fainted, but the roots themselves can take a good amount of abuse. Spinach makes me sad. It rushes through its life and bolts straight into seed stage.

From this evening's calm comes a recollection of how cool and gritty irrigation pipe feels on my hands. I remember how I call back to Dean, "Ready," and we stoop to pick up our opposite ends. We trudge across headland and the aluminum pipe will sometimes graze the outside of my leg, leaving a black smudge. Just the thought of this work wakes me to a certain kind of stiffness.

SAGG POND IS SAGAPONACK'S WESTERN BORDER, the division between us and Bridgehampton, the next town. At its head is Sagg Swamp, a freshwater nature preserve. Here the pond is no more than twenty feet wide, and for the mile or so it meanders south, it becomes gradually wider. Just after Sagg bridge, it opens up, lakelike, ideal for the intermediate boater, about three feet deep. At its southernmost point the pond touches upon a narrow strand of beach, a sandy membrane that separates the pond from the Atlantic Ocean.

In summer, good noses can pick up the pond smell miles away. Newcomers frown and press their finger to their nostrils: "What is that horrendous smell?"

When the pond goes out to play, it exits through the "cut", a trench that in some cases is the result of a storm and high tides. Most frequently, though, the pond is excavated by machine. The alewife, which have waited patiently for a chance to return to the Atlantic, can now scoot through. Hapless crabs are caught up in the current. Empty bottles, plastic bags and the occasional duck blind end up adrift. After the majority of the pond's brackish water has rushed out to sea, all that remains of it is a thick molasses-like substance made up of shallow water, mud and nitrogen-rich goose poop. This, most believe, is the alchemy of that signature smell.

The odor creeps up on you. Like fog, it can hang in midair, nose-high. Many are fond of this smell, as am I; it is orienting. But of course a large part of appreciating the aroma is knowing that it is part of a cycle, and the reek is a temporary by-product of the life established there.

This summer the town trustees dug the pond not because it was too full, with people on Seascape Lane calling about basements awash, but because it was stagnant. Down near the bridge a thick sheet of algae covered the water. Birds walked on the sheet, not just small birds but crows and Canada geese too, curious about the shore-to-shore carpeting.

For the most part, good times can be had when the pond drains. The water can rush out like the flush of a giant toilet. It becomes wild rapid–like and swift currents take shape, snaking toward the sea. Courageous tube riders are hurled into the ocean breakers. Large saltwater fish amass to dine on the tender morels that are swept out with the exiting pond. Surf casters congregate. Less aggressive thrill seekers patter about on newly formed sandbars. Snapping turtles as big as Labrador retrievers wallow in the mudflats, prehistoric reminders of emerging aquatic sea life. Ancient docks and mill dams poke out of the muck. Lost islands resurface. Herons and egrets, American bitterns and dabblers snap up the remaining morsels. When the pond goes out, fish get trapped in disparate pools and osprey crowd the air for the easy pickings.

It so happened that the town dug the cut on a Thursday and by Saturday the pond was as low and acrid as it could be. But Saturday was the full moon, and as is the custom of a local environmental organization, a "full moon paddle" was launched. The group gathers at the northern end of the pond and puts in kayaks and canoes, and proceeds south toward the ocean. When they arrive at the beach, they share a festive clambake and bonfire. The full moon comes up out of the ocean and floods the dunes with light. Then, under the luminous satellite, the celebrants climb back into their boats and head north for home.

But on this full moon, as predicted, a cold front passed through. The sky rumbled once and spit three measly drops of rain. By witness accounts, there was nothing to fear and the evening began without concern. A large group—some beginners, some experienced—waded through a few feet of mud and then set their vessels into the very narrow channel. Though it wasn't a casual kind of paddle, there were birds galore, and the happy boaters knew that once they got to the south side of the bridge there would be more water and less mud.

The cookout was going along splendidly when a few noticed that the pristine summer evening had fallen down a flight of stairs. A nasty wind kicked up. Clouds blotted out the moon as an ominous squall line could be seen building in the west.

The inherent dangers of adventure are belittled by the opportunity to witness nature unobstructed, and humans have been known to risk charging elephants, tornadoes and, as of late, snapping turtles. There are several accounts of what happened next: all include panic and the Bridgehampton Volunteer Fire Department's rescue squad. While a few of the group opted to take cover in a nearby beach pavilion, the majority decided to "paddle like hell for it", "it" being the safety of their parked cars at the northern boundary, not a quick trip on even a nice night. Consequently as the storm worsened, there was a drama on the very low seas.

Many of our storms dissolve in the cool ocean air. Others are pushed north over Long Island Sound, but this storm was right here, right now, on Sagg Pond. It came trucking over Highland Terrace and, like a bear, took hold of Sagg Pond and thrashed it. Of the excursion, those who feared they would become lightning rods on the open expanse encountered flesh-rending bullrushes as they fled inland. Others ran aground in the mud; although the lightning illuminated their location in the driving rain, they could not find their way back to the narrow channel. They abandoned ship and were forced to wade through the notorious suck of Sagg Pond's quick mud. Suddenly the group's theoretical knowledge of the environment was enhanced by images of serpents, eel and reptiles of mythic proportions. The ones who fared the best were the slowest paddlers. At the height of the storm they took refuge under the bridge, clinging so tightly to the concrete columns that they scraped and bloodied their hands.

Over the next twelve hours, abandoned crafts were retrieved from under the bridge and various emergency harbors along the shore. Another canoe was pulled from a ditch two miles north, and it wasn't ever fully clarified how it had come to rest there.

BECAUSE IT IS EASIER FOR A CHILD to understand a picnic than a revolution, Independence Day to me was deviled eggs jiggling and sliding on a porcelain platter; I watched as men in swimming trunks swallowed them whole. Those glossy white boats with creamy matte yellow centers of yolk, mayonnaise and mustard, a paprika flourish—this seemed to me to say, "America!"

Today, I hear the man on the radio reading down the list of all the things to do on this great holiday weekend. He can barely contain his enthusiasm. "And the great thing about the Fourth of July being on a Wednesday, we get two Fourth of July weekends!" Like the bookends are more important than the books.

I don't know how I feel about two-for-one holidays. Something in me wants to see them like a blue moon, something exceptional you get rarely. The extra days, although superfluous, are harmless—pure luck.

But I can't help feeling that we Americans celebrate our freedom more than enough as it is. It's not just the kid who has to keep the watermelons stocked but also the box turtles contending with traffic that doubly suffer the impact of "our" freedom. Not since man tamed the horse has he felt so absolutely free to go anywhere or up anything he wants, no matter what the consequences or the harm done. At Sagg Beach, where that lovely long ridge separates the pond from the ocean, there is evidence of this. On one side of the sand dune is perhaps the thickest and most handsome stand of *Rosa rugosa* in town. On the ocean face, the dune is steep; it crests like the waves that shape it. At the foot of the dune is a deposit of black sand. It is finer, warmer, softer, and if I roll my wet body in it I look like an aborigine. But people in their SUVs keep trying to breach this fragile dune wall. I can count the number of times they have attempted this, making deep parallel trenches, like notches, were it possible, on the SUV gunbelt.

Today I had a chance to watch a man bury his Range Rover in the sand at Gibson Beach. Before they perfected the idiot-proofing option on the 4×4, and before there were cell phones and willing tow trucks, it was not uncommon to see a wild-eyed stranger limping down Main Street toward the nearest pay phone at the general store. Sometimes, however, these characters would see the tractors in our yard and come knocking. I've seen my fair share of desperately stuck cars. I sometimes come upon them already fast in the sand and wonder how they did it. So, when the brand-new, dark blue vehicle roared past me in the parking area, I hastened my pace so that I might see the whole incident from beginning to end.

The truck plunged down the entranceway onto the sand and then hung a sharp left. Rather than follow the paths of others, this driver chose to hug the unstable base of the dune banks. He cut the wheel too hard and I watched as the "unstoppable" vehicle lost momentum. The driver cut the wheel the other way, again too drastically, and the beast burrowed into the sand in four successive rooster tails, completing its demise.

Through the rear window, I could see the driver and his passenger exchanging ideas. At last they must have decided the problem was a flat tire. He got out and checked. This was not what he had envisioned when he bought his powerful machine; this predicament looked nothing like the advertisements. He climbed back in, made a last-ditch effort, and tried to execute a three-point turn. The SUV was now buried up to its axles, and for the inexperienced, hopelessly.

I raced home to get Dean. "Hey, you want to make a quick fifty bucks?" We were back at the beach in under three minutes. Dean approached the scene. A brief conversation ensued; the man got out of his SUV and Dean got in. He rolled the window down, fixed his forearm against the door and leaned out to watch the front tires. He "straightened it up" and, never spinning, never accelerating, managed to make the heavy car light. He made a wide U-turn and went closer to the ocean, onto harder sand. He lined up with the entrance to the beach and paused. The transmission clunked; the car idled a few inches backward. The reverse lights went off and the Range Rover flexed its pretty-boy muscles as it tore faster and faster up and off the beach.

Dean explained that getting the SUV unstuck was too much fun to take the owner's money, though he offered. I thought about something different: not that the driver

got off easy, but that he didn't know the difference between freedom and ignorance.

It is difficult to define freedom, anyway. Is it the pres-
ence or absence of territory? A little further down the
beach, closer to Peter's Pond, I discover a colony of nesting terns. These birds lay their eggs in the little depres-
sions they make in the sand. Whereas some birds employ
height or impenetrable brambles to protect their young,
the terns rely heavily on camouflage and defense. When
I draw near, they launch an air assault: they dive, screech
and poop in my direction.

Small as terns are, they are effective; I watch them
push a great blackback gull—a bird several times their
size—way out over the water. What I also note are the
tire tracks running through their encampment, and I
wonder. I don't think the birds could scare off a chrome
grill and halogen fog lights. So I go home and call a
friend. We return with tomato stakes and a roll of yellow
"caution" tape. With the birds relentlessly on wing, we
erect a fence for their territory and their freedom—and
maybe for ours, as well.

SAGG CEMETERY is about a quarter mile from our farm.
Main Street travels along the west side of it and for many
years, the road on the east side had no name. It didn't really need one. It is all of one hundred yards long, gives
obvious access to Gibson Lane and then bends, circum-
venting the old burial ground before it rejoins with Sagg
Main. About ten years ago the narrow road was sponta-
neously and unimaginatively named. What was once "left
at the fork" is now Cemetery Way.

When I was thirteen, my father suggested to his peers on
the Sagg Cemetery Board that I take over the job of mowing the cemetery's grass. It was an employment I was hon-
ored by and terrified of. But I really had no choice. I mowed
it and because I often procrastinated, I mowed it at the very
end of the day. Many of the stones are so worn by time that
the identity of the interred cannot be determined. And
many more graves are just plain anonymous, with no stone
at all. I think because the cemetery is so old, opening and
closing its earth for deceased residents since the late 1600s,
that many of the buried have no living descendants and
thus their graves tend to be a good deal less manicured than
others. Such resting places are sometimes marked by an
eerie rectangular depression. To a kid, at dusk, little could

be more unsettling than to feel the lawn mower lurch, as it did under me, and descend into those morbid cavities. I barely managed the grass cutting for two seasons before I willfully relinquished my custodial position.

In addition to history and a lot of old stones, our cemetery has a "green", a little triangular space outside the confines of the split-rail fence. It's a more public space with a flagpole and a flag that sometimes someone puts up and a very large spruce tree—the one we light at Christmas. The most recent addition to the green—again a spontaneous one—is a small garden.

The man who decided the cemetery needed some colorful flowers installed and cared for them on his own volition. He planted—and thickly—daffodils and tulips. A few years later, the gardener unexpectedly died, and while spring flowers are always there, those meant to grow in the summer months are now not so certain. The bed must compete with weeds or drought and by mid-June, the little space can look pretty forlorn. Earlier this summer, after the daffodils had finished, two friends and I decided to take the bed over. And we did okay with some larkspur and salvia but not nearly as well as the original designer.

Last Friday, I stopped on the way back from the beach to do some impromptu weeding. It was an exquisite evening, and weeding uninterrupted is as meditative a task as I could ask for. There was very little traffic and I was contentedly lost in thought when the distinguished rattle of a diesel Mercedes Benz drew near.

I know how I must have looked with my back to the car, squatting in the posture monkeys sometimes employ while intently grooming their mates.

The car's electric window whirred down and a lady said, "Excuse me, sir?" It was a sweet voice, high-pitched and strained with politeness, but I am sensitive about being mistaken for a man. When I was six, being called a boy or being mistaken for a son was an honor. Then I emulated boys; I thought they were better than girls. But at thirty-one, if anything irritates me it is a woman who fails to recognize one of her own. So our brief relationship did not get off to a good start.

"Ma'am," I said, pivoting slowly on my heels to face the carload. Her eyes were well fixed with mascara, and acknowledging her mistake, she half-closed them with a prolonged, overtly feminine, quivering blink. The lady wanted to know where Caroline Kennedy lived.

All weekend news vans and dish satellites have lined Dunham's corner. Reporters with cameras and microphones crowd the pebble driveway, and from time to time a helicopter makes a low, invasive pass. And all of this because Ms. Kennedy's brother was killed in an airplane crash and the American public thinks they need a good look at a grieving woman. The one talking at me gestured to the other woman in the back of the sedan. I could see a bouquet on her lap. "We want to deliver flowers."

I like to think Sagg is the kind of place where celebrities, heirs of celebrities, people in witness protection programs, and reclusive writers or painters can live in peace—not so much unrecognized but unfussed-over. And it's not that I am concerned with their right to privacy as much as I am concerned about our town being inundated with the kind of people who flock to their human stars.

CELEBRITY AND BEAUTY AND HIGH-END SHOPPING are often found in the same geographical oasis of plenty. By now, there should be no doubt that the Hamptons is all about beauty. Not just its landscape, bullfrogs singing, ocean, sky and bird beauty, but also its aesthetic component that steps from the train or jitney. I have a friend who worked one summer as a busboy at one of the season's most popular restaurants. He told me this: "Marilee, beautiful people have a job to do. They move differently than us through rooms. They are important. They are the perpetual reminder of books and their covers." But most of us learn either through waiting tables or tending gardens that just as the beautiful can be unattractive on its inside, so too can the ugly be beautiful.

I raise a type of tomato called "heirloom," to many the homeliest-looking specimen of fruit. It does not look, feel or taste like other tomatoes. And the reason is that heirlooms—unlike the prolific and disease-tolerant "Whopper VFT", a true garden performer—have never been hybridized or otherwise adulterated.

Some heirlooms lived in genetic purity, isolated (or so it is claimed) on Amish farmsteads. Others, like the Black Krim or Caspian Pink, were protected or sequestered, behind the wall of Cold War Europe. Hillbilly, a big yellow tomato with an impressive red streaking pattern, supposedly came out of some old southern garden. Aunt Ruby's Green

German is a kind of Granny Smith among tomatoes, sweet and snappy, while Nebraska Wedding is appropriately low-acid and smooth.

With heirlooms, it is hard to know what you are getting, because seed catalogues are notoriously optimistic. What is written in those hyperbolic descriptions is often true, but is seldom the whole truth. For example, Great White is as wonderfully flavored as they say—smooth, subtly sweet, and the pale yellow flesh does look divine sliced on a platter. What the catalogues don't mention is you'll only get about three football-sized tomatoes in an entire season. The advertisements say duplicitous things like "fragile" when they really mean "splits-no-matter-what". I start as many as forty different varieties but end up picking only half of them, if I am lucky.

For all their variety and singularity, heirlooms have other severe drawbacks. Unlike tomatoes that have been selectively bred to produce both great flavor and disease resistance, my tomatoes are vulnerable to wilts, specks and spots. Unlike those that ripen evenly and stay firm, heirlooms don't ship well. There are tomatoes made better by man's intervention: tomatoes that are drought-, cold-, heat-, moisture-tolerant. When I see baskets brimming with uniform red, round fruits at other farm stands several weeks earlier than my heirlooms, I ask why, what am I doing with my incongruous fruit?

I had an art history teacher who believed that works of art should not be considered in terms of their beauty. "Truth is beauty, and surely," Ms. Mancoff added with a tight, ironic smile, "beauty is truth." She was trying to show her students how an artist could take a moment in time and keep it ringing like a tuning fork for a thousand years, but that balanced or even agreeable compositions had nothing to do with real beauty.

So it is with heirlooms, though of smaller sociological impact than art. They do not impress me with their perfect composition and familiar palette so much as they do with their complexity. Like good art, heirlooms are rare, sometimes odd-looking and hard to find. My rows are now nonexistent; vines that won't stop growing wrap from one cage into the next. I must part the foliage with my feet or hands and peer deep, sometimes into the very dark recesses of this plant, to see the pink orb of a Brandywine glowing back.

While I try to be a farmer, these tomatoes keep me in art school. My father shakes his head. He says I must spend more time becoming a better farmer. His rows are straight and his weeds are few. Yet out of my personal jungle I come bearing the unbelievable.

A friend arrived to help me pick. I usually wear my picking basket, part of my attire: an old, stretched-out tee shirt. The hem seam is doubled back toward the sternum. A 100 percent cotton shirt, preferably one that belonged to a larger member of the family, can hold anywhere from six heirlooms to two hundred cherry tomatoes. I needn't set my basket down, only to lose it among the vines. But this week's body-crunching heat proved to be too binding for tee shirts, so my friend and I switched to dresses. She showed up at seven a.m. in a sheer black slip, white pajamas still discreetly underneath. Though she looked fashionable enough, she picked like a machine. A dress with a lot of flirty fabric can hold more than a tee shirt—nearly a dozen "Carmellos" and about four "Mr. Stripeys". Perfectly attired, we went tripping through the vines, plucking, laughing, sweating, and sometimes falling silent.

Heirlooms get your attention. Something about them—only good if fully ripened on the vine, their strange shapes, the way some people react to them with raised eyebrows and alarm—makes me feel as if I am one step closer to what really counts. A longer look at my heirlooms, one preferably with salt, redefines the easy meaning of beauty.

I AM SURE A LOT OF INTERESTING THINGS HAPPENED in Sagg this week. I missed all of them but one—irrigation. Summer has shifted into high gear and left us dry. Our nutritious soil, revered for its ability to hold moisture, now resembles light brown talcum powder. With potatoes about to blossom, it is a bad time for drought. If they don't have enough moisture now, the plants will stress and energy that should be sent to the roots, where little spuds are anxious to take shape, must be diverted for mere survival. If it doesn't rain—or we don't make it rain—there will be a significant drop in yield.

Irrigation is a challenge. Because it interrupts all other farm activities, it is sometimes fun. Wild and unexpected things happen, from slapstick human error to pressurized pipes unhooking and shooting thirty feet straight up in the air. Irrigation is promising the way gambling can be promising. My father says he's made money in dry years. If our yields are up while others' are down, the extra but essential work will pay off.

Like all my siblings, I have been moving pipe since I weighed fifty pounds, the approximate size you must be to leverage one end of a forty-foot pipe. Twenty years ago, irrigation was a real ordeal. It required more people, and thus the conscription of unsuspecting houseguests was commonplace. Most of our childhood friends (though they now claim to be glad for the memory) learned it was a bad idea to sleep over at the Fosters' in times of drought. The closest thing to a Saturday morning cartoon was the outspoken schoolteacher my father hired for the summer. Henry, having come from an innovative, nontraditional educational environment, was always calling, and loudly, for meetings. Halfway through a "move", if things were becoming discombobulated, which they often were, he'd yell with operatic inflection, "I think we need to sit down. I think it's time we talk this over."

There are really no analogies to moving pipe. It comes close to a three-ring circus with its rapid variations of human, mechanical and environmental behavior. But there was always this tangible sense of urgency that made those early, muggy mornings knee-deep in saturated earth feel as if I were shackled to eight others, on the lam through southern swamps.

Lying between two rows all the way down the field was a line of detachable sprinkler pipe. Our task was to move the line while keeping as many sections as possible intact. Communication was crucial. We spread out, one person at every coupling. The last person in the line unhooked the pipe from the pump and signaled, and the rest of us gave a unified tug, theoretically "breaking" the line in pieces.

Sometimes, even after the pipe was broken into a few pieces, water stayed in it. So before we could carry it, we had to drain the water by making the equivalent of a human hill. One end was hoisted overhead and then it was propped successively lower, on shoulders to arms, hips and finally knees. When the water rushed out, the pipeline reverberated. Small people, like myself, could barely stay upright. Then someone would yell "ready" and we began to walk. Walking the pipe was the most treacherous part; coming out of the just-watered rows meant slogging through mud. People fell, chins got whacked, and we would come to a jarring, cursing, messy halt.

When the pipe was finally walked twenty-four rows over, we had to rehook the pieces, which didn't always fit back together easily. We laborers hated this very angry, backward tug-o'-war.

We've since modernized and while the work still entails heavy lifting and mud, it requires fewer people. We can move irrigation more quickly now and generally with fewer errors. Today the only pipe we have to haul is called the "main". It has no sprinklers and is used only to carry the water from the well to a device called the "big gun", "reel rain" or simply "the irrigation rig". Rather than an aluminum pipe running the length of the field, the rig is equipped with fifteen hundred feet of flexible PVC hose, which we tow out using a tractor. At the end of the hose is one giant sprinkler (that's where the term "gun" comes from). At the other end is a steel drum ingeniously equipped with a water-driven turbine. The turbine makes the drum turn and slowly the hose can be recoiled. Every fourteen hours, nearly ten acres of potatoes are satisfactorily quenched. Moving the contraption can be done alone if necessary, but Dean and I have found that together we make quick and relatively light work out of what, to the uninitiated, appears daunting.

Too dry is preferable to too wet. Irrigation is the result of what is basically the lesser and more manageable of weather evils—drought. There is also, in irrigation, a certain amount of chivalry; the plants are in distress, and we, shiny-armored farmers, are coming to their aid. When water starts flying, we bask in our gallant status. We stand breathless, hot, muddy, looking out over the crop. We listen to the rhythmic *tisk* of the water-breaking arm and take credit for saving the field that was just hours ago struggling to stand. In a matter of days the foliage will have closed the rows, and the watered field will simultaneously go into the visually impressive stage of full blossom.

Sometimes when we're out moving irrigation, I notice how many early morning joggers there are. And I wonder if they see and consider the possible benefits of my dirtier rendition of an aerobic workout. Their faces twist with the agony of compelling their not-yet-in-shape early summer bodies, "keep going, keep going, keep going." I wonder, as the spandexed traffic increases, if the joggers notice that my job distracts me from the pain associated with a fitness regime. Every day I use my hands, arms, back, shoulders, steel toes and vocal cords. I sprint, I tug, I exert strength I didn't know I had. When I am done, I haven't run an agonizing five miles, but my mind and body still hum with that coveted sense of accomplishment. I have earned my breakfast in a more literal way.

Unfortunately, irrigation has a very unappealing side effect. For all the sense of purpose, peace of mind and shapely muscles I might gain, I lose bits of my collected mind.

We have two rigs going: one takes ten hours to complete a run; the other is closer to twelve and no matter how carefully we plan, Dean or I must take turns with sleeplessness. When it's dry like this, no matter how hard we work, water can only fall so fast and, to avoid losing time, we have to keep irrigation running around the clock. Summer nights are spent sleeping, waking, checking the guns every four hours, moving them when necessary and returning to bed. Sleep deprivation, like tequila, is an experience to which no one is immune. Giddiness slips into tyrannical fits of futility, since it is easier to make mistakes. With scorn beginning to fester, I look at the field and acknowledge an ugly fact: in local real estate terminology, potatoes aren't worth the very dirt they grow in.

ON SATURDAY, summer officially, quietly, rainlessly arrived. It was dark by the time Dean and I had finished our irrigation work. I went into the house, where my father, who has already moved enough pipe in his life not to move any more, wanted to know how everything went, and I told him "fine," for if it hadn't, I wouldn't be home yet. I plunked down across from him and asked when it was going to rain. He reminded me that today was the first day of summer, with a long way to go. As if testing my mettle he said, "The weather you have on the solstice is the same you'll have until the next."

WHEN YOU ARE PART OF A FAMILY that spans five generations of farming on Long Island, you're likely to have
potatoes in your blood. To me, the common vegetable,
though taken for granted, is also sacred. If my family sits
down to a dinner without potatoes, my father's plate
may be full but his eyes sweep the cluttered table.
"What, no potatoes?" and the meal is denounced as incomplete.

The round white potato has seen us through markets
good and bad. It has been held in storage, firm and sprout-
less, as we've waited for the price to rebound, if only
slightly. It has withstood droughts and floods, and has
yielded adequately despite nature's adversities. We are in-
debted to the potato and eating it at every meal is just one
way of showing our undying appreciation.

One spring, when I purchased seed for a potato other
than a round white, I acknowledged ahead of time that this
was as risky as serving Idaho russets. My move was not just
an insult to our local industry but also a gesture like turning my back on the steadfast and fine-eating friend we've
found in the "Allegheny", "Superior" or "NY 103". It was
a digression from the tried and true, and even to me, always
in search of the strange and the colorful, it did feel a bit
like betrayal.

"You think people are going to eat those ugly things?" was my father's response to the seed pieces for a variety known as "All Blue", really closer to purple. Unlike the potatoes we were used to, these were longish and unattractive, lumpy, thin-skinned.

But we planted them anyway. I was confident of an emerging market for purple mashed potatoes and Cliff was innovative and generous enough to let me exercise my own naïveté. The truth is that these pretty violet spuds, mashed, set up like concrete, but people like the taste and the "babier" the better. So I dig my crop by hand. While many will tell you that a potato is just a potato, excising these colorful tubers from the dirt is like unearthing treasures; they are radiant and Easter-eggish.

Since that first uncomfortable spring, I now have the confidence to ask that we clean out the planter, change the sprockets and plant blue potatoes, purple ones, red ones, yellow ones. When "my" potatoes infiltrate mealtime, my father is both courteous and curious. He always tries one. He mashes it down with his fork, adds no butter or salt—that's the true test. His response is usually along these lines: "I don't know if they just look like soap or really taste like soap." He pushes the blue-gray potato to the edge of his plate, "they do nothing for me," and takes one of his own whites from the bowl. My only defense is that people other than my immediate family seem to like the colorful spuds. Their loyalties, of course, do not run so deep.

This year when I was told All Blue would not be available, I decided to plant fingerlings. Again the seed pieces were met with skepticism. But where taste, looks and storability fail, culinary trends suggesting economic reward protect my insolent defections. "Fingerlings," I said, "are worth big money." In reality, after harvesting by hand a yield that is nowhere near as enormous, these potatoes should be expensive to buy.

Fingerlings are not long and straight like a fine lady's fingers, but gnarled and bent—as if they belonged to a laborer who has smashed them, abused them, worked them so hard that they close up arthritically.

A few weeks ago, when I dug the first hill and found nothing but deformed, peanut-sized shapes, I was regretful. I considered that maybe this was one potato ill-suited for Sagg's otherwise perfect growing conditions.

I came back from the field, wanting to show and admit my error to Dean (being a brother, he still finds my missteps humorous). But since he wasn't yet out of bed, I looked at my pathetic palmful and reached my hand through the cat door to place the mutants inside. I left them where he couldn't miss them. And not only did he see them, but he mistook them completely, as did his girlfriend, who went about cleaning up the potatoes as anyone would clean up a cat's accident. She threw them outside, rug and all.

Two weeks later, the fingerlings had some size to them. I dug them, piled them in little half-pint boxes and witnessed anew how deviation from the norm breeds interest and sales. But this was not half so satisfying as when I passed through the kitchen and my father announced, "They're damn good eating."

IN AN OPTIMISTIC MOMENT the laundry gets hung out to dry. As the day progresses, the humidity persists and the clothes get wetter yet. When it's nearly dark, in the foggy, metallic light, the line with its heavy towels and sheets sags like a suspension bridge decorated with bannered regalia. In summer's very obvious decline, time becomes oddly abundant. Orioles return to the pear tree, not for the blossoms this time but for the fruit that rots and has yet to fall. Weeds finally make it through the bluestone driveway. The grass that had died in the shade of the elm becomes green again, just in time to receive the same tree's deluge of papery leaves.

This year, I notice that the tomato skins are thin but tough. They take up the moisture and split. Something in their demeanor seems unnecessary and resentful. By mid-August my shoes take on a certain high odor. As smells go, it's sweet in a low register. The smell is of all the tomatoes I picked, but didn't keep or throw far enough away, and subsequently stepped on.

With things as they are here, with an economy that is increasingly geared for people with thick wallets, it is easy to overlook some who arrive here seasonally, not to spend money but to make some, if only a little. They are not the waitresses, college-student nannies or masseuses that are part of the luxury economy, but migrant workers, who may have pulled the sweet corn you ate at dinner. They should not be mixed up with undocumented aliens who are equally, if not more, common than fieldworkers in agricultural regions. Increasingly the line between the two groups is blurred, but I am speaking specifically of crews that follow the most abundant or labor-intensive harvest, up the coast from Florida to Maine and back down again. They live this way almost entirely, with plenty of recognizable "camps" but no permanent home.

When you are a migrant worker, your life is partially conscripted; there is one person who, though he does the same fieldwork, wields more power. This is the crew leader or contractor, the person who shuttles the crew from farm to farm. Not unlike other businesspeople, this individual has more pull because he has more responsibilities. He assembles the eight- or ten-person workforce and then makes all the arrangements with the farmer concerning salaries, living conditions, length of employment. Most of the workplace dialogue is simplified because the crew head speaks in the interest of all. For his crew, the contractor has endeavored to secure work, housing, transportation and sometimes food. He is thus entitled to a fee or, more simply put, a portion of the laborer's paycheck. Any businessman can see the rationale that exists between the laborer and the contractor, providing all transactions are fairly carried out; it is efficient and legal, basically. But nothing could be further from horseback riding and tennis than this: a financially strapped, unsettled life. It is an existence so tight that a church on Bridgehampton's Main Street serves migrants hot lunches every day.

Potatoes, though a waning crop for the area, still require a relatively large seasonal crew, and the transient workers who spend their summers here come to grade potatoes. And while our grading operation is run by workers who live here year-round, there are days when a crew, hired by another farmer, isn't packing, and so they come to us to pick up a little extra cash. In general they are a younger bunch, and when they are working for us the trailers get loaded with potatoes more carefully and quickly.

Each crew has its own set of rules. Some contractors permit workers to work wherever they please if the farm they are technically hired to work on doesn't need them. This extra cash is a private windfall. But more often the arrangement is less profitable. The worker we hire for the day is not a free agent but is "borrowed" and is still obligated to give his contractor a cut of his pay.

One afternoon, long after the grader was finished, one such man was sitting on the steps alone. He explained to me that he had nowhere to go, but since I knew where he was living I offered him a ride. "No," he said, "I can't go back there." He stood up, came listlessly down the steps and took his bike away from the loading dock. "I already went home, but the guy who's, you know, in charge, rolled my stuff in a sheet and threw it outside. He said I can't stay there no more. But he didn't tell me why . . . and I say he can kick me out if he wants, but he got to at least get me on a bus back to Florida. He brought me here. He got to."

I'VE HEARD IT SAID THAT WEEDS ARE JUST PLANTS we've
yet to find a use for. Weeds are more and more a part of
today's popular cuisine. And I know people who believe
that weeds should be worshiped for their unique flavors
and obscure medicinal applications. However, there are
those of us who can't help but hate weeds. My father is
practically insulted when a salad plate of purslane or dandelion arrives. To think that he should eat his enemies.
Our family regards weeds as costly nutrient vacuums that
crowd the intended crops, robbing them of moisture and
sunlight. I have had to contend with morning glory chok-
ing out potatoes and phragmites overtaking the asparagus. Yet I am sometimes awed by the vivacity weeds ex-
hibit. If only humans could develop the deep roots of
ragweed, the immortality of foxtail—to die and live
again, to show no scars, to grow big and strong in spite of
the farmer's determined hand.

A lot of weeds are in full bloom right now. One last
hurrah before the winter sleep will promise them a place
in next year's garden. Open space, the fallow neighbor of
cul-de-sac development, is home to the most marvelous
stands of goldenrod. In the late summer light, the weed is

a sea of yellow fronds. And the goldenrod's pungent flowers provide a favorite food for migrating monarch butterflies that make neglected properties forgivable. I see
smartweed, the spidery opportunist that has nestled down
into the dormant lilies. Its pin-sized pink and white seed
scatters. It is an unwelcome hitchhiker. Pigsweed, no
doubt the king of all weeds, rises like a gothic spire, pink
and green and gaudy, dwarfing the dying sweet corn.

And then there is burdock. The root of the burdock reminds me of an eel, long and greasy, and yet it anchors itself so securely that only by placing both hands near its
base and using your whole body as a counterweight can you
dislodge it from the soil. The root is the edible part of burdock. I have julienned it like carrots and steamed it. Allegedly, if cooked properly, the root is digested and metab-
olized as a natural tonic, helping the body cleanse itself.
But it is not this purifying root that elevates the burdock to
the category it shares with thistles and milkweed—a category of weeds that are like master thieves, not necessarily
an asset to the community but fascinating to have around.

The burdock produces a burr, a spherical, spiky seedpod.
When the plant has finished out its season, the burr dries up
and is easily dislodged from its stem, and thus a lone plant
tucked behind the garage is enough to turn a cat into a
walking ball of Velcro. In the pasture, burdock turns a
horse's mane into a prickly ridge and a well-groomed tail
into a tangled club. Hunters lament burdock; it takes more
time to get the burrs out of their spaniels' coats than it takes
to shoot and pluck ten pheasants. Burrs caught in the arm
of a wool sweater become part of the permanent weave.

But burrs have their allies. A woman once confided in me how she sculpted furniture with them. She made fainting couches for her dolls to nap upon. Burrs are also a safer, bloodless way of curbing the mouse population. Stuff their holes with burrs, and you deter the rodents from nesting. But burrs for health and household chores are not half so interesting as burrs for styling hair. This is what a friend and I discovered one warm autumn afternoon when we were six and more inclined to experiment with interesting material than to imagine a plausible outcome.

The burdock patch was located in a relatively abandoned corner of our farm. It had grown up and eventually walled off a tiny Homosote shack. On that day Sarah and I had set out to make the shack our private fort and while the stand of burdock was good protection, we would need an inroad. We began an ambitious trailblaze but were only a few yards into the established jungle when both of us became fascinated with the way the burrs attached themselves to our fine hair. Despite our tomboyishness, we took a few moments to enhance ourselves cosmetically.

We cupped our hands and ran them up the dried limbs of the burdock, collecting the burrs by the handful and then pressing them into our hair. We patted and shaped; our stylish minarets grew strong and defiant. The sensation alone was enough to please us, for the towering mats that now swayed from our scalps were like brand-new, involuntary body parts. When we walked, the burr towers bobbed sideways so that our steps felt unsteady, and our small bodies were tugged along by our hairdos' momentum. With our towers leading, we went dancing into the kitchen. My mother raised her eyes from her paper and we greeted her scrutiny with melodramatic curtsies and stifled laughter. While she did not flinch or scream, her eyes narrowed and became fixed and she pointed to the door. My mother was and is a champion of spontaneous and unconventional creativity. Had we crossed the line? We exited, the laughter drained. Sarah reached up for her bangs, her little fingers prying for a purchase, but there was no hair, only solid and impenetrable burrs. It was then, in the sudden twilight of our grave concern, that we felt the conical masses to be much too heavy and unbearably itchy.

Banished from my house, we retreated to Sarah's. We took an assortment of combs from the bathroom and for sustenance, a half gallon of ice cream from the freezer. We crept through the backyard and disappeared into her tree house. By this time our scalps were burning; the persistent tug and teetering that had originally delighted us was now a horrid, yanking encumbrance that at any moment might tear our hair from our scalps. For the remainder of the afternoon we sat with our heads bowed, each picking burr by brittle burr from the other's hair. Our arms became stiff and little bits of burr crumbled down our backs, adding more successfully to our punishment. We winced and whined and gritted our teeth. We were fuming and silent as the ice cream slowly melted. What took us twenty minutes to do up took us almost four hours to undo. And when the work was done, we sat listlessly surrounded by the dust of the scattered seeds and a blanket made from the broken strands of our frizzed hair.

To this day I don't have much hair. There are little barren or nearly so spots that I sometimes attribute to trends in caustic hair dyes. But other times, when I'm snipping burrs off the cat's back, I believe the thinness has more to do with that wanton summer afternoon when I was six.

Fall

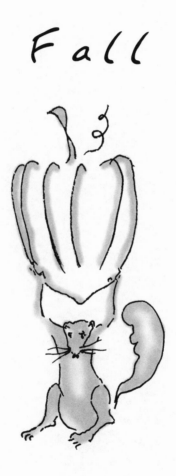

SKIMMERS LOOK LIKE DINOSAURS, pterodactyls cartwheeling on the tips of leathery wings. In the sinking sun they resemble spinning jacks—invisible, then silver—until they turn again and come at you, black as taut velvet. Although the skimmer's flight is not random, it moves like paper in the wind, flirting and then, by a subtle shift, frozen. Necks bow and five fiery mandibles slice into the water's still surface, showing a wake, as a blaring trumpet shows a sound.

Once summer has rounded the bend and its longest days have been wrung out, regardless of the season's vitality, you begin to notice night slipping back for longer, sleepier stays. As I pedal away from Sagg bridge, my back is to the sun. A night heron heads in and I stop and turn to watch its silhouette descend. The bend in the road and the sway of the electric lines frame the sun's final antics. The field corn, a little dry but full-grown, is challenged to reach up to the sky as if to touch the end of the day.

Though I'd like to deny the images and ignore the sensations, fall has begun. I noticed it, despite the temperature, when I stepped onto the deck and heard a rustle, a brief, low-pitched whistle and then a "splat". The pears are beginning to drop, and this is my first hint that the growing season's final stage has started. Now, all that has been born begins to decline. With this comes relief, however, as we dig our first crop of potatoes and find them larger and more numerous than expected, with a nice tough skin. For all our extra labor, we feel cautiously rewarded. Our most recent rain has been used up and irrigation must start again—but for now, not at a desperate pace.

No matter how the phone-toting masses behave, August does not belong to them. August belongs to the insects and to the bugs, to the lowly buzzing ones you slap and shoo, to the floating dancing swallowtails and to the ones who cause you to peer fruitlessly into the maples and whisper, "Shhh. Listen." The cicada makes an amphitheater of the tree. It starts up gradually: just one, somewhere in there, becomes deafening; the branches must vibrate, the roots must take a firmer hold.

With the exception of a few car alarms and the cicadas, it was a quiet week. A brief spell of warm, dry weather meant the oats and rye could be harvested. And then it got hot. Even in Sagg, a land normally blessed by ocean air, the weather was miserable. The breeze died along with the zinnias. Graham crackers went limp in the moments it took to open them. The birds panted, their feathers ruffled, their beaks agape in a desperate gesture. The chickens made holes in the shaded, cooler ground beneath the trees. Weather like that is what makes the beach a topographical treasure. There is no saner place to be than up to your belly button in the ocean, with the salt stinging all your scratches.

A friend arrived at our farm today and commented that Sagg Main is like a strip mall of farm stands. I suppose it takes being from somewhere else to notice the colorful fall abundance of this little place.

The ants have just gotten their wings, and the guinea hens call attention to what would otherwise be unremarkable specks floating just a few feet above the grass. The birds, flustered and crazy as they seem, are marksmen with their beaks. The flock behaves like ballerinas at warm-up, going through their different parts. All the hens go in different directions, up on their extended toes, grabbing ants from midair. Dragonflies swarm at the edge of the asparagus patch for a meal of maiden aviators. The light that makes its way between both barns is not the same this afternoon. My eyes know that there has been a change. When autumn comes to us, the humidity is less pervasive. It's like looking through a filtered lens, crisp but distorted. This afternoon is yellow.

GORILLA IN A RAIN SUIT. She's my scarecrow without im-pact. I made her from an old mannequin's torso and the mask of a giant primate. Since proper legs were hard to come by, her body is held up with a single fencepost. The legs of her foul-weather gear are thus empty and at liberty in the wind. Beginning at the ankle, the breeze gradually lifts the scarecrow's yellow trousers. A thin leg is stretched outward. This exaggerated step that goes nowhere is like the slow-moving dance I once saw a drunk lady do in Memphis. I have tethered the scare-crow's arms outward, in theory to gesture a continuous "shoo!" The sleeves fill, billow and flip. The gust slips past, and her snapping arms cease. In the moment that follows, my gorilla looks dejected, as if her offering to some obscure deity has been rejected.

Her expression, which consists chiefly of permanently bared fangs, is no longer forbidding because she can emit no roar or growl to match it. The deer are accustomed to her empty threats. In the scarecrow, I imagine a downhill transformation. Originally, she liked this job, out alone as sole protector of ten acres. She, like many farmers, shared an exhilarating but fleeting sense of importance. But it wasn't long until she understood that if the deer stopped fearing her (and they had), the world would go on; it would buy its lettuce elsewhere. I do not know if it is my mood or her looks, but my gorilla and I are inseparable. Today, I think she is sneering, and this is new to me.

I'd rather avoid her caustic temper but as we look over the deer damage, like business partners watching sales and productivity drop, her white eyes roll. Although I am worried about the deer, I suspect it is me, and not the predators, that she is fed up with. We look at the lettuce, so carefully raised and transplanted, only to have the deer nibble and tear the middles from each head all the way down the row. And now my gorilla, my ally, the monster of my own creation, finally makes her feelings known: "If you only had a fence, like any proper farmer would . . ." She begs the question of how I would feel to spend my nights in such futility. How could I fail to notice that the wind, which makes her lively in daytime, dies at sunset. She is right about everything. Wordlessly, we sink into a mutual funk.

Deer never used to be the trouble they are today. Seeing one was rare, and my heart would go pitter-patter as the fleeting vision, a graceful and dainty creature, slipped into the swamp. Deer lived in the woods, scouring the forest floor for a tender shoot here, a wild blueberry there. But as their habitat was built on or fenced off, a few brave deer struck out for new stomping grounds. They stumbled into Sagaponack—a virtual paradise. Deer, like all animals, flock to where food is abundant and predators few. In Sagaponack, with so many fields and such a vast choice of foods, they eat like kings. The buds of a nice merlot, raspberries, arugula, acorn squash, tomatoes, corn and gladiolas make an exceptional meal. Like many who have chosen Sagg for their home, deer prefer the ocean breezes to the stifling woods. They can get away from biting flies and saunter all along the unobstructed pond shore, sipping the water, cleansing their palates as they visit one farm after the next.

To deers, my fenceless and plentiful gardens are the Shoney's of the great Northeast. Like a drove of out-of-towners, the deer gravitate toward my cheap, all-you-can-eat buffets. They spend the day bedded down in the adjacent rye field, and at dusk they come over the hedgerow. By their tracks, I can tell the herd hesitates on the headland. The buck snorts and checks the air for trouble. My gorilla is nothing but an ill-trained hostess, listless and timid. Gradually, the hungry diners come in, happy to find their own tables. Some like the beans. Others hit the sunflowers or paw up a hill of potatoes.

I could probably live with the herds if they were more frugal. But the infuriating thing about deer is they are like Goldilocks to the tenth power; they sample everything, and while they don't necessarily eat it all, they make much of it unmarketable. It is not until they have done substantial damage to the vegetables that they finally decide the cantaloupe looks just right. They devour them. In the morning I can see how their front teeth scraped out the sweet flesh and left the rinds as empty bowls. Farmers call deer "rats with hooves".

While it is true that new homes have caused some of the initial migration, farmers have probably accelerated it, not only with their crops but with field corn. For many farms, field corn has replaced grain as a rotational crop. Corn, because it grows tall, provides more shade, thus inhibiting weed growth. The corn's complex root system also promotes good drainage and, even after harvest, the roots and stubble of the remaining stalks help hold soil in place. The following spring when they're plowed under, the stalks continue to break down, replenishing the land with both nutrients and organic matter. Unfortunately, this practical crop simultaneously provides the deer with a shelter they can both eat and hide in. Not only have the deer found a practical alternative to the woods, but corn is an extremely high-energy food. While the majority of our local crop goes to Eastport Feed where it's made into duck, horse and chicken pellets, the deer get first dibs. Even after the field is harvested, the combine has dropped enough corn that if they don't mind sniffing around, they can have a dependable winter snack shop.

The stable food supply has contributed admirably to the health of these herds. Seldom will you see does with just one fawn; they now have "litters" of two, and both usually survive. Such would not be the case in less accommodating environments. While most herds average between four and seven deer, we have some as numerous as twelve. I have seen several herds come together, like it's Thanksgiving—thirty or more scattered around a seven-acre lot.

The difference between deer and our other pests is that deer are not crop-specific; they eat anything. And though spraying garlic and hot pepper oils might save the smaller gardens, it's not feasible for larger acreage. Temporary solar-powered electric fences are a good line of defense but again, they can be expensive and time-consuming to maintain.

While I have frequently been mad enough to imagine myself attacking a deer, wrapping my arms around it and viciously biting its neck, I don't think I could actually shoot one. I am gun-shy, so I use bottle rockets. But I have applied to the DEC for "nuisance permits" giving me the right to let specific hunters take a deer from a specific place even if it is out of season. I have seen freshly killed deer and held the flashlight as it was butchered. The combination of blood and hands and organs steaming in the cool air is something I can't easily forget. But it doesn't double me over with pity, for the meat is going to be eaten. Some people like to stay in touch with their hunter-gatherer side, just as some conscientiously go to great lengths to disguise our omnivorous condition with tofu hot dogs and soy burgers. I don't have trouble with either point of view. I take issue only with those who cannot see themselves as part of this problem, such as the homeowner who builds an eight-foot fence around his estate to protect his ornamental shrubbery but gives no thought to the displacement it causes. Or the one who is comfortable with the fact that he can purchase a loin wrapped in cellophane, an animal that has died in similar if not more violent circumstances, and yet curse and protest the "barbaric practice" of hunting.

Deer are the biggest and wildest animals we have in these parts. While they cause landscapers heartache and nasty car accidents, no one has put forth the idea that we saddle them up and ride them. Reindeer polo could be huge.

So much about Hurricane Floyd made me fear him. Even the name sounds like a pedophile. As we got ready for the blow, Norman, one of our work crew, stood momentarily idle. He looked folded into his raincoat. His arms stuck out rigidly. The slicker was so big and awkward it made him look like a child who'd rather get wet than wear it. The hood, which was made to snap onto the collar, had come unsnapped and was riding awkwardly atop the baseball cap Norman chose not to remove. But Norman has worked for my father always, at least longer than anyone else, and he knows all the routines well: planting, harvesting, drought and storms. He has experienced a vast number of farming-related scenarios that are outside his conventional assignments.

We were looking at a shed with no foundation and, like Norman's rain hood, it seemed destined to be separated from its designated place. The shed had once been a corn crib, a tall, simple structure with airy slats where corn left on the cob could dry. Later, when we had no pigs or cows, it was home to many hornets and rodents. The building, now without function, nevertheless had nostalgic charm. It was partially renovated but its completion was never made a priority and now, with winds of uncertain force threatening, the shed was resting on the I-beams of a homemade house-moving trailer. It was too high to haul inside and too unstable to withstand the approaching storm.

Standing with us was Slim, who is not a young man and is so tall and narrow that we question his balance. He stood silent and assessed the situation. Never one to waste words, Slim did not confer with me or Norman. He assessed the problem from the confines of a raincoat that, unlike Norman's, was too small. The rain trickled down his exposed wrists and face. He stared at the vulnerable shed, straight at the hole that will eventually be a door, and he began to laugh. Slim's laugh is like that of a goldfinch in flight, only much, much lower. It's singsong that comes unexpectedly from the basement.

Norman—halfheartedly, slowly—ducked in and out of adjacent barns, looking for rope.

"Why?" I asked.

"To tie it down." He looked at me with seriousness, brought his shoulders up, closing some of the gap between his slicker and its hood, and in his traditional manner issued an amused "Goddamn." He has a way of dragging this two-syllable epithet out. It brings humor to what might seem like dire situations. "I don't believe it will amount to much," he drawled.

The entire day was spent like this—in thorough preparation for a big blow. It really wasn't until late in the afternoon and in some cases not until the next blustery morning that we felt comfortable accepting that Floyd was going to be merciful, at least to Sagaponack.

It was the time of year and the storm's proximity to the autumnal equinox that added to our anxiety. Summer had been blasé, with only a few good thunderstorms. The ocean was ominously warm. Some corn blew down; some tender vegetation was burned by the ocean's salt. That was it for Hurricane Floyd.

The storm, minor as it was, seemed to pull into its wake the most glorious days of the year. A Saturday afternoon had been imported from Vermont, and a couple who had just been married on the beach were ecstatic, not only over their madly-in-love condition but by the light and how, as they took their vows, monarch butterflies steadily drifted overhead, migrating south.

THIS WEEK, under a full moon, the cat puked up a fruity-looking mess and went off her food. The same animal that normally lingers under a mildly affectionate gaze scooted sideways and fled outdoors, flicking her tail in disquiet. I have been told that weeds pulled under a full moon will not come again. Fall begins on Friday. Fall, spring's contrast, is just as powerful, though generally considered a sort of coming-undone. Whereas spring evokes preparation for life, fall is for selecting caskets and checking one's pulse.

The elm lets her leaves go early. And though I welcome this twilight and the return of eastern standard time, I do so with the sense that it is always too soon. I cannot stand the lost photosynthesis snapping like piles of thin porcelain beneath my feet. With the garden going down too, I rationalize taking the afternoon that should be spent pulling tomato stakes, chopping and turning vegetation under and spending it elsewhere. I work to reclaim an almost unknown entryway into the rear yard where a patio made from old bricks has been taken over by bittersweet, smartweed and wild geranium.

IN SAGG YOU WILL NOT FIND A SOUL bemoaning the solitude that, like a weather system, settles in between each Monday and Friday in fall. While I pick pumpkins, I think it is probably best to do nothing but watch the "nothingness" of limited light and late September.

I go to the beach when the west is the color of a faded bruise, its normal sunset show pressed down by an overcast evening. Four shapes of a family come together, one by one their bodies plinking into the sea.

I inspect the lightless facades, the empty houses that cannot hear the difference in the sound of the surf. A calm sea, when a clean wave builds silently, collapses in a sharp piercing peal, one violent slap that reintroduces the hush of order. I feel hurricanes churning far away, evident tonight in the small but consistent roil on the beach. The last flocks of sandpipers hurry along and pip curiously, perhaps speculating on that same arrhythmia.

WE ARE LUCKY TO HAVE AN OCTOBER LIKE THIS. Just as March is about wind and July about humidity, October, when it behaves, is all about sky. The clouds seem to have been set on a giant glass table and we, curious children, are privileged to stare up from underneath at their flattened bellies. This is when everything from cornfields to half-built houses stands in stark, awkward contrast to a blue backdrop. Great swarms of blackbirds feign collision, as by the hundreds they shrink up, twist together and roll through imaginary obstacles. Unified to behave as one, they are pulled from the air and plunge into the phragmites. Their cackling falls silent. Then, just as suddenly, they explode back out and upward.

THERE ARE TWO KINDS OF BLACK GOLD. The first is found in the desert, in the arctic and deep under the sea, in very hard-to-reach places.

In Sagaponack black gold is not oil. It is dirt. And while dirt can most accurately be considered a long-term bargain, it is often depicted in an undesirable light. "Cheaper than dirt" or "older than dirt". You have to be an oinking pig to justify your love of it, unless, like my family, we grow our livelihood in it.

Tonight I talked to an acquaintance who is in the business of growing grapes. Though Sagaponack is perhaps best known for the October onslaught of ubiquitous, lumbering potato trucks, trucks that loom in front of your car like elephants on a mountain pass, this small fertile area generates another massive harvest. Grapes, when compared with potatoes, seem like nectar from a flower.

Grapes are about running along hillsides with muses and centaurs.

Potatoes are about sleigh rides in subzero Siberia.

One day last week I saw the grape workers assembling. The sun was just turning from red to yellow and the grass was sopping. The morning shimmered. And then the dozens of pickers vanished from sight. As my truck whined its way up the hill and began to gather speed on the flat, each endless row of trellised vines was one at a time momentarily open. There, I got a glimpse of little clusters of busy hands and bent necks. By the end of the day they had picked nearly thirty tons of cabernet, which also means that each person individually picked an entire ton of grapes.

But grapes, unlike potatoes, are less about yield and more about quality. Whereas a potato farmer needs to find a balance between quality and quantity, the fifty-five-acre vineyard in Sagaponack is constantly examined for color and size from the winter pruning to the fall harvest.

Even with this kind of attention, some grapes are more rigorously cared for than others, producing the estate selection that arrives on your table. Every grape that goes into making that prime bottle won both the beauty pageant and the talent contest, whereas the others, in order to end up bottled, had only to make the finals. The Wolffer Estate in Sagaponack picks an average of three and a half tons per acre, or approximately ten thousand cases of wine. A potato farm digs about twenty to twenty-five tons to the acre, roughly enough French fries to kill an army of marathon runners.

Farming, no matter what is grown, has many schools of methodology and grapes are no exception. The fellow who picks his grapes by machine in California will tell you that way is the best way, and he'll have scientific (or economic) proof to back up his opinion. In Sagg, grape growers believe that harvesting by hand provides a final grading opportunity and is more gentle with the product. For those who doubt that good wine can be created in a cooler, maritime climate like ours, there is this reply: what Sagaponack lacks in heat it makes up for in consistency. Our weather climbs and descends slowly; grapes are usually permitted a long and healthy handling time, which results in ideally ripened fruit. This year, with our questionable summer but exceptional autumn, is being cautiously touted as the best year yet.

And then there is the black gold factor, our not-just-good but incredible soil; it is our foundation and future.

LAST WEEK CAUSED SKEPTICISM on the sundress front. Shorts got stuffed away and wool sweaters were pulled from their mothball dens. I had to wear a hat all day and my head began to burn—not from heat but from the involuntary response of wildly jostling the itchy cap about whenever I had a free hand. To make matters worse, my hair was eventually worn and crinkled like straw bedding. Late in the afternoon, when the sun was mostly down, Dean and I filled the last of the potato trucks. We climbed out of our respective vehicles and met between the two, as is customary, to discuss the logistics of who would drive what home. Dean had been listening to the weather and I could see he had the word "frost" on his lips. He bent down and poked his hand, a primitive but reliable soil thermometer, into the freshly dug field. I lifted my hat and let the cool evening touch my irritated brow, and then I too put my hand on the soil. It was cold. Cold still from the previous night, after a day full of sun had been unable to warm it.

And so there is a frost, a slightly early but plenty welcome icing. As I drive to work the next day, I note it in all the usual places. The lawn at Minden, with its impeccable lattice pattern of neat mowing, is topped by a white shag carpet. And the golf course too, white as dandruff on a navy blue blazer. Dunham's Corner, perhaps Sagg's lowest spot and where my cole crops grow, is dusted like snow. Local cauliflower, flavorwise, will now become optimum.

Yellow jackets crowd into anything ajar. Flies slow up and seek out warm nooks. They creep into them like particles of benign dust and wait. From time to time they will emerge on a warm winter day, crawl up the window glass and make a spectacle of their longevity. I swat them dead with a dried-out Christmas garland.

THE FROST AND THE AROMA of sweet rotting apples that the chill launches into the air are perpetual and customary. Now the swamp reminds me that Jack Frost is an arsonist. From lush canopies he has made hot, undousable colors that curl the leaves. To me, this is the most exquisite yet desperate time of year.

The garden is a less spectacular series of quick, searing fires. The adamant tomato vines turn blood-red and scream out loud. The tops of the plants have become charred and black but the lower parts and even some of the tomatoes are still alive. The blaze has been only in the rafters, leaving the house standing but most likely unsafe.

I watch as a squirrel buries something just ten feet from the side porch, in what is unquestionably enemy territory, that of our terrier. There is a constant stream of squirrels in and out of the cornfields. They take entire ears away with them, greedy but determined to get the groceries home.

It is said, and largely believed, that when squirrels work so hard, a long, cold winter is on its way. It's interesting that we, who consider ourselves the most intelligent of creatures, continually revert to watching the so-called lesser ones for clues about our future. You will never catch a squirrel peering over your shoulder as you read the paper and fret about the price of home heating oil.

YARD SALES ARE A PERVASIVE VENUE HERE. They flourish in the spring and again in the fall. Such sales are a way to bestow for a price a lifetime's accumulation of junk and treasure on another. It is not necessarily true that quality will define the item. Usually, it is the potential owner's expectations that set the price. Two kinds of people regularly go rummaging through stuff that is in reality just one day away from the dumpster. One is the savvy, oft-in-disguise antique dealer, who has his eye and his pocketbook both firmly in hand. This shopper knows exactly how to spot and resurrect a forlorn masterpiece. The other type is the individual who roves without clear intention, buying what she fancies, not by definition but by intuition. I don't go to yard sales, but it is not because I do not like them. I don't go because I am generally toiling between the hours of eight and noon, the most propitious time for second-hand shopping.

Out here, yard sales are especially interesting. The often gently used goods and the frantic atmosphere of nothing else to do on Saturday combine to make the yard sale a scene of wanton shopping. Sometimes it's the experience and not the purchase that provides the excitement.

I know a woman who bought a ceramic bird while traveling in Europe. It was dirty, but she envisioned that behind that stubborn film, the porcelain bird's haughty, marginally placid expression was one only a master's touch could have made. She snatched it up. Instantly it became her most wonderful possession. Peculiar and beautiful, the bird sat on her lap on a train through the Alps, in taxicabs of Germany and on London buses. Always resting near, clutched especially close on the flight home. But the bird *was* dirty and within hours of her return, the traveler dunked her find into a sudsy bath. As she turned it over to rinse, there on its pedestaled feet were three factory-stamped words, "Hecho en Mexico". This bird, no longer a treasure from a Renaissance workshop, was probably a result of NAFTA. Surprised but not saddened, the woman immediately placed the bird on a prominent kitchen shelf where it still imparts bemusement along with its south-of-the-border feathers.

Of course this kind of shopping doesn't only happen at flea markets or in somebody's front yard, in a crowd of worried elbows and vying wallets. It can happen in one unscheduled afternoon among the bittersweet and ryegrass that customarily grow up around the edges of older farms.

I know a man who recently became a farmer. Typically farmers are made by generational osmosis. But there are other ways, too. The most expedient is to take all your money and invest in seed, land rent and secondhand equipment. Ted grew up on Hedges Lane. He has been everything from a motorcycle repairman to a plumber, a spelunker and an underwater welder. He's worked for farmers, on and off, for the past fifteen years, and for my brother the last four. Next year Ted intends to grow beans, just to start out, a little side hustle. When he saw the forgotten tractor rusting in a corner of a barnyard, he identified it as "a find". If it would run, he said, it was the perfect size to handle two important pieces of equipment, the cultivator and the bean picker. It was a Farmall 706, a machine made in the 1960s. In tractor years, it was middle-aged. But with tractors, as with people, middle age is a relative condition, and there was no telling what kind of life this tractor had led.

Many more practical people would look at this machine and see only faded paint and flat tires—a mechanical relic, better left to rust. But Ted gazed at the tractor and saw a "cream puff" merely dressed down. He found the owner, a farmer who had since gone into real estate, and with cash in hand, Ted made his best offer.

Later that afternoon with an air compressor, two sets of jumper cables, some fresh gas, a can of Sure Start, and a towrope if all else failed, Ted and I set out to claim his prize. In twenty minutes he had it running. In twenty-one, the power steering came to life. The brakes, the three-point hitch and the PTO all worked. A little slower to cooperate was the throttle, but this could be mended, like the hydraulics, leaky seals and headlight. Hearing the motor run smoothly, Ted found high range, put the Farmall into fourth gear and struck out for home. He hurried, as one might when he knows deep down that he's gotten a steal.

IT USED TO BE WIDELY BELIEVED that certain people be-stowed with magical powers could control the wind. The directional gales were kept by priests in tightly lidded jars. Others stored the wind in the hollow cane of bamboo. It could be exchanged between parties in a leather bag. Sailors purchased the invisible but critical momentum from bewitched old women who claimed to tie the gusts into special knots.

Of course, with the belief that one could create the wind came the understanding that sometimes the wind fell into the hands of unsavory creatures. Stormy weather was the work of demons who, when drawn out to sit by the warmth of a fire, would have water thrown on them, thus extinguishing the wind along with the flames.

Today we are aware of the impotence we moderns have against the elements, but are not complacent. A leaf raker beats his fists into the air as an expression of severe frustration. A failed kite flier may fall prostrate to his knees. A farmer tests the wind with a sniff and a vane, even while accepting its omnipotence.

Winter came gradually on Saturday. As the afternoon progressed, each northerly gust brought in another piece. Late that night it collected itself and howled around win-dows, finding those left open. Blowing playful drafts about its new quarters, it heralded morning with a dip in the temperature. Feet recalled their vulnerability, as did ears, those two parts seeming to suffer first and separately from the rest of the body. Their complaints would go unheeded until later when they warmed and said, "I told you so", with burning throbs.

Snow squalls tapped down on brittle leaves. There was the smell of fireplaces at work. There was the chance to press a cold hand upon an unsuspecting cheek.

What remained of the crops—pumpkins that will not be carved, squash that will be cellared, tomatoes too nasty to pick—will go down finally with the weight of a honed chopping disc. What I left is briefly regretted; I may even get down from the tractor to consider that last ripe-looking remainder before committing the final act of destruction.

My mother and I are inspired by the prolific pumpkin patch and endeavor to carve as many pumpkins as possible. As the snow squalls make us, against our will, think of Christmas, we are inside the tin barn with an electric handheld jigsaw, carving up free-association jack-o'-lanterns—modern art, a plunging blade speeding through orange flesh. They will finally rot. Most will do so on our doorsteps, though some will be placed in trees or deep in the underbrush where, if the thieves miss them, they will slowly diminish into their candle-blackened cores and vanish with a wicked grin.

SUNDAY WAS THE FIRST DAY of pheasant-hunting season. This means that all seven of Sagg's surviving pheasants will be keeping an especially low profile. Though I've never been one to protest the sportsman's way of keeping wild populations in check, I'd rather see camouflage gear in *Vogue* than bloodied and behind me in the coffee line. I pity our poor pheasants; thanks to a booming population of foxes, the elegant birds are under siege all year. In my garden I have witnessed this. When a fox hunts a pheasant, flight is the bird's defense. The bird runs out of the hedgerow with a young fox on its tail. The pheasant takes off and the inexperienced hunter leaps. The canine's body contorts with the effort; it twists, jaws snapping, but it misses and hits the ground in a humiliated heap.

On the other hand, when a human hunts, flight is the bird's undoing. Its colorful plumage contrasts with the stark gray November sky. The gun cracks, the frantic flutter ceases and an obedient dog rushes toward the downed game.

Deer season is also open, at least for those who hunt with a not-so-primitive bow and arrow. If you're like me and decide to venture out into the far reaches of Northwest Woods to take in the exceptional foliage, you run the risk of cardiac arrest. I think I am alone but suddenly out of the bush, twenty feet in front of me, a hunter stands up and says, "Don't worry, I won't shoot."

My family is not inured to this season, but neither is it immune. Every November, with the changing leaves and the far-off pop of a shotgun, I remember how Dean was stricken by an affliction called "pheasantitus". My brother got it every year, without resistance, and missed school on the first of November, the first day of pheasant hunting. And while it upset me that I never caught anything so exotic, I accepted my no-hunter health.

Pheasants used to be as populous as crows. Sagaponack's let-alone terrain once provided these birds with perfect living quarters. They lived comfortably in the numerous ditch rows and overgrown fields. They practically crowded Smith Corner, the thirty-acre lot in west Sagg. It was a rarity to look across a farm field and not spot a pheasant strutting his stuff, occasionally pausing from his impressive display of color to peck just-planted cover crop out of the ground. Like my seasonally truant brother, many of the residents here used to hunt the birds. Then, they were well fed and healthy and made good eating. More than that, to an ambitious sportsman, pheasants are an elusive quarry. They are clever, quiet unless startled, and endowed with a natural camouflage. To bring a pheasant home for supper was rewarding proof of a competent gunman and a capable dog. By the second week of the season, it was common to hear talk of a favorite dog who was so loyal that she'd sooner die than come back empty-mouthed.

Such a dog would tolerate a painful share of catbriers to retrieve birds that hadn't even been shot.

What has happened to the pheasant season isn't a mystery. I am sure there are a number of people happy to know that one more sport involving guns is locally on the wane. But in Sagaponack, pheasants haven't been hunted into the present scarcity by human beings. To the contrary, these birds have had their habitat invaded by predators less notorious but equally dreaded—crows, foxes and seagulls. Pheasants have lost territory to human encroachments as well, unintentional predators who, by building a house or manicuring a fallow field, expose and cramp the smaller, less aggressive creatures. How we hate to admit that the swimming pool, patio and tennis court are akin to a smoking gun.

A FEW WEEKS AGO I watched my father harvest the field corn we raised on Smith Corner. It was nearly night, and the combine looked like an alien vehicle traveling in a force field of dust and lights. The very next day a fleet of excavating equipment arrived. It's no exaggeration to say that the landscape of Sagaponack has changed overnight. Curiosity and concern govern the facial expressions of those who ask, "What are they doing to Smith Corner?"

It hurts to see the earth in piles and a new road down the middle of what once was farmland. It's like deface-ment. My father has farmed Smith Corner for forty years but never owned it. Of course, we knew what was likely to take place there. With the help of the Peconic Land Trust and various anonymous contributions, some resi-dents on the west side of the pond orchestrated the pur-chase and preservation of some of Smith Corner's acreage. When the remaining portion came up for sale, the heavy price made their repeat performance unlikely. Good news: the prospective buyer had plans for keeping the majority of the acreage open and would build just one house.

Smith Corner is considered marginal farmland. It's low-lying, and if there is too much rain or the pond gets just a little too high, the land tends to fill with water. For many years my father attempted to make the most of the property, even that which was not arable. So the lower half was used to pasture twelve fire-breathing steers. These cattle had a virtual wilderness to roam in, good food and ocean views. All the same, they preferred to travel. Once they made it past the snares of the barbed-wire fence, they became invisible. The cloaking device they came to rely on was the sorghum-Sudan grass planted nearby. They would duck into a field along Bridge Lane and not surface again for days. But we got plenty of irate phone calls. The steers had plowed a shortcut through a manicured back-yard. They'd nearly run over a bewildered homeowner. They fell into swimming pools.

One of the most memorable pasture breaks took place in the early 1970s. After a week of extensive searching, we found the escapees in Wainscott, the next hamlet to the east. A crew of makeshift cowboys took off to sur-round them and drive them home. The posse, a moving corral, was made up of four on horseback, two in pickup trucks, a jeep, and a motorcycle. It took the better part of an afternoon, but all of the herd was moved three miles back to Smith Corner. Events like this eventually con-vinced my father that the steers were more trouble than they were worth. He continued to rent the property but, rather than wrestle with the whole parcel, he let the pas-ture be and farmed potatoes on the higher half.

Another critter soon arrived at Smith Corner. Whereas the cattle meant a full freezer at least, this new one—the golden nematode, a microscopic pest that invades the roots of potatoes—diminished yields. Although the nematode is a complex parasite, the governmental agency in charge of eradication turned out to be more lethal. If a farmer's land was identified as infested acreage, he was held responsible. Compliance became antithetical to the imperatives of growing a crop. The farmer was required to plant nonhost crops or varieties resistant to this pest. No dirt was to leave the acreage. All equipment entering or exiting the field had to be steam-cleaned. My father endeavored to do what was permissible, shadowed by a small but persistent bunch of government agents. Now, as dump trucks haul tons of so-called infested topsoil away to make room for a new mansion, I too ask myself, "What are they doing to Smith Corner?"

In its earliest days, Sagaponack was thought of as a sort of wild hinterland. I once read of a man who lived in Southampton Village and, when ordered to reprimand his own son (by publicly whipping him), refused and moved his entire household here. While you couldn't disappear in Sagg, the thinking was that no one came looking for you either. This was a place where one took care of oneself; neighbors were out of earshot. Geography alone granted maverick status. That same geography, three hundred years later, is turning us into a kind of high-end suburbia. And there is now an active core of citizens amassed in the name of Sagaponack. They want Sagg to be an independent, incorporated village, rather than a feckless protectorate of Southampton Town.

Those who currently envision Sagg as a last outpost of modesty and simplicity are not those who have ancestral connections here. Instead, the charge of overcrowding is being led by relative newcomers. And who can blame them? The injustices Sagg has suffered imply that our local government is either inattentive or spiteful. It is probably true that nothing could have stopped multimillionaire industrialist Ira Rennert from building the largest house in America in Sagaponack. But it was wrong that as the entire population of Sagaponack begged for our local government's support or even intervention, the opposite occurred. Rather than represent their constituents' interests, Southampton Town's officials shrugged their shoulders. The 65,000-square-foot fortress on Peter's Pond was approved and is now in the process of being built.

The Rennert mansion is not the only cause of local discontent with its government, but it has become a galvanizing factor. Another factor is the condition of our public roads. Speed limits do not take into account that on any given Saturday, our roads must allow as many slow-moving farm vehicles as weekend speedsters. These roads look as though they have been shelled; most of the pavement is scattered on the grassy shoulders. And the potholes are so big that Sagg is famous for them. Now there is the proposal to turn Poxabogue driving range—a tiny, already nonconforming golf course located in a residentially zoned area—into a family recreation center, including night golfing. As residents cry "foul", town officials insist that this "improvement" is consistent with Sagg's character.

So, incorporation has its attractive side. For one, the perception exists that because we all live here, local residents have a united understanding and vision as to what is good for Sagaponack. Unfortunately, there is no proof that a smaller, neighborly government could be any more effective in stopping "progressive" growth. In opposition, there is the sense that the nearer and more intimate the government becomes, the more meddlesome and con-trary it may turn out to be.

For me, I do not look out my backdoor at yet another subdivision. I can still see a farm, the unqualified essence of my life. And while I understand that my opportunities as a farmer here may diminish, I also recognize that I can adapt to some changes. More obstinately, I have learned that there is a difference between those who seek only a place to play on the South Fork, in contrast to those who make a life here.